ISBN: 978-1-955184-06-9

Contents

D of the Devil   V

Chapter 1   1

Chapter 2   11

Chapter 3   20

Chapter 4   29

Chapter 5   39

Chapter 6   48

Chapter 7   56

Chapter 8   67

Chapter 9   77

Chapter 10   85

Chapter 11   91

Chapter 12   100

Chapter 13   110

Chapter 14   116

Chapter 15   126

Chapter 16   133

Chapter 17   141

Chapter 18   147

Chapter 19   155

Chapter 20   163

Chapter 21   174

Chapter 22   181

Chapter 23   187

Epilogue   193

About Josie Max   199

D of the Devil

I swore I'd never love the man that forced me to be his bride.

<u>Selena</u>

I made a deal with the Devil.

I stepped foot into the kitchen hoping to grab a snack, but my hunger soon died as blood pooled on the black-and-white marble counter. The talented executioner and head of the most powerful mafia family in Chicago, Domenick Satriano, stood there wiping red splatter off his cheek. He had spilt blood. My father did nothing as Domenick casually took my hand and led me to his car as if we were meant to be.

I should have run that day, but something ignited inside me as his dark eyes gazed down at me. He pulled me toward him and I willingly came. I was weak to his touch. He told me he owned me, but I wanted to break free. Trapped inside his gilded cage, all I wanted to do was run. Every night, he used his wicked hands to break me. Every inch of my tender flesh burned after he finished. He explained it was a matter of time until I willingly came to him. My damaged heart kept me fighting his dark games.

What happened when Domenick grew tired of the fight and used his talent on me?

<u>Domenick</u>

I had been watching her for years.

Her round, green eyes stared up at me with such innocence it was hard to control myself. She's perfectly sweet and ready to be devoured. I couldn't wait to taste her. To hear her cry my name. And I wouldn't let up until she admitted she was meant for me.

She thought she could fight me. No one said no to me. She didn't realize my heart had been scorched and burned so long ago, there was almost nothing left of me. She was just a promise from long ago, and I never broke my promises. But once I inhaled her sweet scent, that promise turned into obsession.

Chapter 1

S elena

A cool breeze blew, sending wisps of chocolate-brown strands to tickle my cheeks. I pushed my hair from my face and pulled my jean jacket tighter. Early June in Chicago and warmth was only a dream.

My eyes shifted down Lawrence Avenue to watch the last glimmers of the sun slip behind the buildings.

Shit. My dad was going to kill me.

Thanks, Camela. My bestie swore our quick trip to visit her boyfriend, Danny, wouldn't take long—she lied.

She also swore his hot friend would be hanging out with us. He was there, but as for hot... Well, that was left for debate. He was good-looking, sure, but he was also drunk. The guy kept trying to feel me up, and I finally had to nope myself out of there.

Now my dad was going to lay into me for being out in the dark. Ugh, he acted like I was a child and not a twenty-year-old woman.

I graduated from high school two years ago, and I had been working at his shop ever since. My dad needed me.

I nibbled my bottom lip. What was he going to say when I got another job?

I had an interview at an upscale bakery tomorrow. The pay was great, and it came with benefits. The job offered more than my dad could ever provide for me.

This potential job would also pay for culinary school. It was my dream to work in a world-class restaurant one day. I had just bought a book on spices and had been devouring it.

I knew how my father would react. He'd pretend to be happy for me, but there'd be hurt in his eyes. I was all he had.

I slipped around the corner and down a row of dark brick buildings. I had grown up here; this was my neighborhood, and I loved it.

My father ran his convenience store a few blocks up on Lawrence, and everyone knew him. He was like a father to a lot of other kids here, too.

Did I grow up with money? No, but I got everything I needed. My dad worked his ass off to make sure he cared for me. Even when I was twelve and Mom left us, Dad showered me with enough love to make up for what my mom couldn't provide.

I slipped my key into the door to our building. Opening the glass door, I stepped into the tiny lobby and shook off the cold.

I took my time and went over to the row of metal mailboxes that lined the wall until I came upon the one labeled *Alba*. Opening it, I frowned. There weren't any envelopes, but something was in our mailbox.

The sender had wrapped the unusual package in white cloth. My arm hesitated for a moment as I reached for the object. It was long and thin, but quite hard. I removed it, and when I did, I saw a tag hanging from the top.

Mr. Alba. Time to pay. - D.

What the hell? Something inside told me not to unwrap the thing.

I ran up the building steps with only the sound of creaking wood and my heavy breathing filling the air.

My hand shook as I unlocked the apartment door. When I finally got inside, my dad was sitting on our worn gray couch, watching the local news. He had a thing for the anchorwoman, though he always denied it whenever I teased him.

"It's going to warm up tomorrow," my dad announced without turning his head, and he pointed to the television. "High of seventy, they say. Maybe we can take a walk by the lake tomorrow, like we used to. With a Chicago dog and a pop."

I leaned back against the door and held the package to my chest. What do I say? *Dad, a guy named D put this in our mailbox, and I don't think it's a lollipop.*

"Selena?" He glanced back, his thick, dark brows pinched together. "Sweetie, what's going on?"

He stood and came over to the door. "Did something happen? I told you to be home before the sun sets. You never know who's walking around—"

I shook my head. "Nothing happened to me."

Ever since I told him about what our landlord, Mr. Banks, did to me a few months ago, my dad imposed a strict curfew.

Mr. Banks stopped by the apartment looking for rent, but my dad was at work. He insisted on coming inside to "inspect" the apartment. What could I do? He was the landlord, so I let him inside.

Only, the thing he wanted to inspect was *me*. He kept lifting my skirt when I turned my back to him. Then, he pinned me against the kitchen counter.

I feared what would have happened if my neighbor, Mr. Faretti, hadn't stopped by. It seemed when Mr. Banks came inside, he left our front door open, and Mr. Faretti was concerned when he saw my door ajar.

My dad told me never to answer the door when I was home alone and not to be out late. As much as I didn't want these strict rules put on me, deep down, I felt safer with them in place.

"Then what's wrong, Selena?"

I held out the package. "This was in our mailbox... and it's addressed to you."

His eyes widened as he took the cloth-covered item from me. After a moment of staring at it, his gaze flickered up at me. "Maybe you should go to your room for a few minutes."

Our apartment was small. We had a tiny galley kitchen, a living room with a table by the window for eating, two small bedrooms, and one bathroom that barely fit one person at a time. It wasn't luxury, but it was home. When we needed privacy, we would ask the other person to go to their room, or we would go to our room.

"No." I pushed my hands onto my hips. "I'm an adult, Papa."

"I don't think this is something you need to know about."

My jaw tightened. It was time to tell him the truth. "We live under the same roof. I'm an adult now, even if you don't want to see it. So much so that I have an interview at the bakery tomorrow; you know, the fancy one in the Loop. Pretty soon, I'll be making enough money to help pay the bills. I need to be a part of things around here—the good and the bad."

He didn't react as I expected.

Instead of a fake smile or disappointment in his eyes, he just nodded as if I mentioned we were low on milk.

"You're okay with me getting another job?"

He smirked. "It's about time. I love you, sweetie, but you've got to get out there and stand on your own two feet."

My shoulders sagged. I had been worried about nothing.

He stared at the package in his hands. "This is something I never wanted you to find out about..."

He went back over to the couch and sat. I followed and turned off the television. Facing him, I grabbed his hand, cupping it in both of mine. "I love you, Papa. It couldn't have been easy to raise me by yourself after Mom left, and now it's my turn to help you. To show you how much I appreciate all you did."

"Don't worry about me. Once you make enough at your new job, I want you to promise me you'll get your own place. Maybe get an apartment with Camela."

"Where am I going?" I waved around the room. "That's a long time away. Whether you like it or not, Papa, you're stuck with me." I smirked.

"Always with the jokes." He chuckled.

I reached up and cupped his cheek. "It got you to smile, and that's all that matters."

"I wish that were the case," he mumbled.

"Who is D?"

"You don't want to know."

"You're right, I don't. But he's telling you it's time to pay, and based on how you're reacting to that note, I'm guessing you don't owe him twenty bucks."

There was silence. My father could be stubborn when he wanted.

"Papa..." I thinned my lips.

"You're too much like your mother."

I never liked it when he compared me to her. She was selfish and only cared about having fun. Too bad I wasn't fun enough for her.

"I'm not her. I won't ever leave you."

"You will. And when you find out what happened, you'll run. And when you do, I won't blame you."

I hated how my father kept this from me. Whatever was hurting him, he had no one to turn to. He spent every day at work, and even on his days off, he'd check stock and go over accounting.

His parents died before I was born, and his brother was killed when he was a teenager. It was just us now.

"No, I won't. Please, Papa, you're scaring me."

"Fine. But don't say I didn't warn you..." He took a breath and blurted out, "D is Domenick Satriano."

I gasped and let go of his hand. "Oh my god. D, of course. Why didn't I put it together? The Devil himself. The head of the Satriano family. How does a mob boss know you?"

"I never told you this because you were hurting enough when your mom left. But she didn't just leave us... She took from us too."

My brows shot up.

"She cleared out all our savings—even the little I had tucked away for you to follow your dream and send you to the best culinary school. But your mother killed that dream. I worked so hard just to cover the savings she stole. To make rent."

I hated that woman. I wished the Devil was going after my mom, not my dad. My mother deserved his wrath; Dad didn't.

"Why would she do that?"

My father reached for me, holding my hand. "She had met someone. He convinced her to leave and take the money so they could start a new life together."

"How do you know that?"

He let go of my hand and reached for his wallet on the table next to the couch. He took out a folded, yellowed envelope and handed it to me. "She left this for me to find when she abandoned us."

I opened the delicate envelope that had so many creases from years of wear. The sight of my mother's handwriting was like a slap to the face. I remembered how she wrote, and that seemed a strange thing to remember, but I did.

In the entire letter, there wasn't one mention of me. Nothing about her daughter.

"I never wanted you to see that."

"Did she leave anything for me?" My voice wobbled. I shouldn't care, but it hurt to know I meant nothing to her.

My father only shook his head. I didn't know if I was more upset about my father dealing with the mafia or the fact that my mother never loved me.

I straightened my shoulders and pushed my mother out of my mind. If she didn't care about me, then I didn't care about her.

"That still doesn't explain how you know the Devil."

"Last year, I was close to getting enough money to actually buy a condo in that place over on Bryn Mawr. You know, the place I pointed out to you?"

It was new construction, and I thought Dad just admired the modern aesthetic. I didn't realize he was going to buy a condo.

"The landlord said he knew a guy who could get me early access to a great unit. Told me since I'd been such a good tenant all these years, he'd contact the guy. I gave him a fifty-thousand-dollar down payment to show I was serious. Only... there was no guy. The landlord took the money, and without that fifty K, I can't afford a condo."

"That's bullshit. He stole your money. Did you go to the police?"

"Of course I did, but they said they couldn't do anything about it since there was no paper trail. Meaning, no contract signed and no emails or texts or anything. Just my word against the landlord."

"We need to pack our bags right now and leave." I stood, waiting for him to get up. "The landlord has repeatedly proven that he's sleazy."

My father's head fell in his hands. When he finally lifted his head, he looked as if he had aged ten years. "The rent for the shop was raised last year. This is the only place to live that's affordable, Selena. The only places available for what I can afford are in terrible neighborhoods, and I won't let you live there. You deserve better."

I sat back down and turned to him. "With my new job, we can find a place together."

"Let's say we do that. Then what? D will still find me. Where do you think I got the fifty K from? With the raise in rent to the shop and our landlord, Mr. Satriano has given me enough time. As he wrote, it's time to pay. The man owns the city. There's nowhere to run."

"When do you have until?"

If Dad owed him today, there'd be men here instead of a package.

"Friday."

That was two days away. There was no way we could get enough money in that time.

"Okay." I nodded, trying to come up with anything I could to help. "We, uh... we leave. Leave the city. Go to the middle of the country, like Idaho or Nebraska. Somewhere he can't find us. We spend tomorrow packing and then head out."

My father nodded, but I could tell from his frown he wasn't reassured.

After a minute, he unraveled the package. I gasped when I saw what was under the cloth.

It was a knife. Not a kitchen knife, but a dagger with a leather-bound handle. But it wasn't the knife that frightened me... it was what was on it.

Dried blood.

Chapter 2

Selena

His smile was hypnotic, captivating, as I felt the warm blood drip down my arm.

He adjusted his collar—white, crisp, and spotted with red dots.

"An apple is all I wanted." My words felt mechanical as they left my mouth.

He tilted his head. And the way his eyes slid down my body, I knew I was in the wrong place at the absolutely, positively worst time.

His gaze felt like fingers sliding across my skin. My toes curled. I didn't know why I mentioned the apple, as my hunger died the moment I stepped into the kitchen.

I considered baking an apple pie, my dad's favorite—something to cheer him up before we set off on the run.

But a man I had never met before stood in my way. I never would have imagined that taking a break from packing and leaving my bedroom to bake would change my life forever.

The sight burned into my retinas was seared deeper than any acid, and no matter how hard I tried—not even pulling out my eyeballs—I could not escape the horror of what I'd witnessed.

The blood wasn't the worst part... it was him, Domenick Satriano.

How he casually stood there with a butchered body at his feet. It made me wonder if I had fallen asleep while packing and was having a nightmare.

It was no dream, just my horrific reality.

I never thought about someone being beheaded before now. How much the blood splattered. Or how odd a head looked unattached to its body.

The moment felt cold. I should run, but, much like that head on the chipped Formica counter, I felt detached. It was as if I were floating above all that was happening and not a part of anything.

I could feel myself get lost in his gaze as he stepped closer. It was like he had some sort of control over me, and I couldn't resist it. His voice was like honey, sweet and thick as he spoke.

"I'm sorry you had to see that, Selena," he said, his hand reaching up to touch my cheek. I flinched at his touch but couldn't pull away. "But it had to be done."

As he spoke those words, I knew that something terrible had happened. Something that I was now connected to, and I didn't want to be a part of it. But Domenick's eyes held mine, and I couldn't look away. I was trapped.

He stepped closer, his body brushing against mine. I felt his breath on my cheek as he leaned to whisper into my ear, but my father stopped him before he could speak.

"My daughter's not a part of this, Mr. Satriano. Please, let Selena go." My father stood as tall as he could.

But he was no match in height to the man who held me captive with his dark glare.

Mr. Satriano's nostrils flared as he inhaled, causing a dimple to appear on his stubbled chin. "That's better."

A shiver ran down my spine as his deep voice rumbled. He was exquisite, with perfect, chiseled features that were only offset by one tiny flaw—a scar just below his left eye.

Even that made him more attractive. So much beauty controlled by such a dangerous mind.

My father's brown eyes flickered over to me.

Was I to say anything? Ever since he told me about owing money to Mr. Satriano, I was afraid. I had heard terrible things about the Devil. And he never got into trouble for the monstrous acts because he owned the cops and the politicians in Chicago. And now the mob boss had his eyes set on my dad.

How could I live without my dad? He was everything to me.

What was happening in our kitchen was bad. One wrong move or word, and I suspected Mr. Satriano would do to my father or me what he'd done to the man with no head.

I stared at the head on the counter and realized who it was. The landlord.

As disgusting as that death was, a tiny part of me felt relief. I never had to worry about running into Mr. Banks again.

"Do what you want to me, but leave my daughter out of it. She didn't know about our deal."

"I don't make deals, Mr. Alba. A deal suggests you had a say in it, and you most certainly did not. It's time to pay." Domenick removed a white handkerchief from his breast pocket, dabbing his brow.

Another drop of blood dripped from the ceiling, hitting my cheek with a wet *plop*. I wanted to wretch, but I swallowed the bile rising in my throat. I didn't dare move.

Domenick reached over with his handkerchief and wiped the drop from my face.

"I thought I had until tomorrow... That's what you told me."

Dropping the handkerchief at my feet, the Devil walked over to our refrigerator and opened the door. "You should feed your daughter better." He sighed.

What? Why was he talking about me as if I wasn't here?

"Of course, Mr. Satriano. I'll get her whatever she wants."

Domenick shut the refrigerator door and turned to my father. "When your landlord told me how you were planning on leaving town, I had to come see for myself."

How did Mr. Banks know? My dad wouldn't have told him anything. I didn't even tell Camela.

"And based on the moving boxes and chaos everywhere, I'd say your landlord was right."

"Look, Mr. Satriano, I was going to pay you, but I couldn't get it all by—"

The Devil held up his hand. "Please, spare me the lies. I know more than you think." His gaze flickered to me before returning to my father.

My dad's head lowered in defeat. My heart pounded while my mind scrambled to think of a way out of this.

"To hurt my dad would be a bad business move." I had no clue what I was saying, but it was something to stall, I guess. But, despite that, it caught Mr. Satriano's attention.

He turned toward me. Part of me felt relief that he was no longer focused on my dad, but the other part was frightened.

I swallowed as the Devil walked over to me. The sound of hard-soled leather shoes pressing down on blood and god knows what else made my stomach churn.

His gaze slid down my body as if I wasn't wearing a stitch. I couldn't imagine he found me attractive in my stretched-out black leggings and worn Free Britney tee.

But the way his gaze raked in every inch of me, he either wanted to tear off my clothes or burn me alive. I suspected it was the latter.

"And what would you know about my business, little dove?"

I had to force myself not to roll my eyes at his pet name. *Remember, Selena, he will murder you with a smile on his face. Don't piss off the Devil.*

I glanced over at Papa, who shook his head, using his eyes to plead with me not to do what I was about to do. But I had to do something. I figured if I fucked it up with Mr. Satriano, then I was dead. But if I did nothing, then my father was dead. Either way, someone died.

And I'd rather it be me.

"My father's respected around here. He's had a business in this neighborhood for decades. He's like a father to some and a friend to others. If you kill him, you'd turn an entire neighborhood against you."

I wasn't wrong.

His dark eyes narrowed—he didn't like what I had to say. Shit. It looked like there would be another beheading in this kitchen, and it would not be my dad.

"You're smarter than I thought, little dove." His voice was low and smooth, sending shivers down my spine. I tried to steady my breathing, knowing that any sign of fear would only make things worse. He stepped closer, his breath hot against my cheek.

"But don't think for a second that I won't do what needs to be done. Your father owes me a great deal of money, and I intend to collect." He traced a finger down the side of my face, making me flinch.

I clenched my fists as anger boiled up inside me. "You won't get away with this. The police will catch you."

He laughed, his grip tightening on my chin. "You think the police scare me? I am untouchable. I have connections everywhere."

I gritted my teeth, feeling helpless. He was right. The law would never be on our side, not when it came to dealing with him.

"But you forget, little dove, I am not a man to be trifled with. I am not afraid of a few angry neighbors; in fact, I find it thrilling to have an entire community against me. It makes the victory all the sweeter."

He studied me for a moment, then looked at my father. "I made an exception for you, Mr. Alba."

I let out a breath I hadn't realized I was holding. He would not hurt us... at least, not today. I smiled at my father, who grinned back.

"Ricco," the Devil called out.

A man appeared behind me within seconds. I jumped and saw the large man with ink crawling up his neck. How did I not hear any of them while I was in my bedroom? Those noise-canceling headphones I wore while packing worked better than I thought.

"Yes, Mr. Satriano?"

"Clean this up for Mr. Rohon Alba. Restock his refrigerator, and make sure the man has clothes befitting of him."

My eyes widened. Something wasn't right. It was one thing to let my dad live, but giving him food and clothing too? The Devil must want something in return.

"Th-thank you, Mr. Satriano, But all I ask is a few more days to get you the money—"

Domenick held up his hand while his eyes focused on me. "Consider the debt paid."

What? The hairs on the back of my neck rose.

"We will pay, sir. I promise. I'm getting a job and—"

He grabbed my chin and pressed his fingers into my cheeks, forcing me to look up at him. "You are not getting a job, little dove. The only thing you will need to worry about is doing whatever I say."

Heat crawled up my neck as I stared at his lips. For a moment, I wondered what he tasted like.

His fingers slid down until he wrapped his hand around my neck, and I felt my nipples harden. Ugh, how fucked up was it that I was getting turned-on right now? I could just hear Camela giggle, "You've got issues, Selena."

"To make sure you don't run, you're coming with me."

I shook my head. "No, please."

"That's my daughter, Mr. Satriano; take me instead."

Domenick let go of my neck but grabbed my arm. He probably assumed I'd try to leave, and he assumed correctly. There was no way I was leaving with him.

"As I said, I'd make an exception for you. This time, you get a choice. Either I can have Ricco do to you what I did to your snooping landlord, or I take your daughter as my bride."

Marry him? My eyes slid to my dad. The look on his face told me everything that was going on in his head.

My father opened his mouth to speak, but I stopped him.

"Take me, Mr. Satriano. Just don't hurt my father."

Chapter 3

D omenick

I observed her wide, innocent green eyes absorb the darkness outside the window as the car turned toward my home. We just passed the gate, and though she was trying her best to hide it, I knew Selena was scared.

And she should be. I was the head of the Satriano family. Ever since I could walk, I'd been surrounded by fear, blood, and lust. It was in my blood to take. And if I gave anything away, it had to be earned.

When you gave things away, that was just a signal that anyone could take you.

Just like I took Selena.

And when the time was right, I'd take her pussy too. She'd taste sweeter than the ripest peach.

What she didn't realize was she'd be begging me to fill her. She put up a brave front now. The girl had spice, and I'd be lying if I said I didn't get a thrill from watching her fight.

My cock got hard when she told me no back in her father's kitchen. God, I wanted to fuck her right there. When it came to women, I was usually more in control, but something about Selena made me ache for her pussy.

I shook my head and gazed out at the pebble-filled driveway. Selena was just a transaction, nothing more. She was just something to keep for a while until the real debt was paid.

A debt no one knew about but me.

We came to a stop, and the car door soon opened. I got out and ran to the other side, pushing my butler out of the way to help Selena out of the car.

I held out my hand, but she refused to take it. Normally, I'd be pissed about the slight, but it was different with Selena. A thrill ran from my heart to my cock, and I cracked a smile.

"I can get out of the car myself," she said, jerking her head back.

The wind blew, causing her silky chocolate-brown hair to flutter. Thoughts of twisting it around my hand caused my mouth to water.

"Take Miss Alba to her room, and make sure she has everything she needs."

Ricco nodded and directed Selena toward the door without touching her. He knew how I felt about anyone touching what was mine.

She folded her arms and sneered at me, "Taking me to your dungeon?"

I ignored her childish rant and turned my attention to Ricco. "Is Elba here?"

Ricco nodded. "He's in the kitchen."

I shook my head with a smile, "When isn't he eating?"

Elba was one of my four brothers. I was the oldest, and he was the next oldest. The Satriano brothers—as we were known back in our old neighborhood growing up—were notorious for doing stupid stuff, like lifting cars and shoplifting from stores.

Kids do dumb things, and we were obviously no exception. Until one day, I was arrested, and my father couldn't afford to bail me out. He went to the notorious crime boss, Angelino Cardoni, but everyone called him Angel. When the Angel swooped in, problems were solved... though, usually, it was with blood.

For some reason, Angel took a liking to me. He bailed me out on the condition I come work for him. I was thirteen, but I learned from a young age what true power looked like.

Power required patience and getting close to the people who required being brought down. Angel taught me more about life than my father ever did.

My father loved us in his own way. But when my mother died during childbirth with our youngest brother, Luca, he changed. Her death ate away at my dad, and he took it out on all of us, but especially Luca. Whenever he'd go after my brothers, I'd get in his way. I took the punishment meant for them, and especially Luca's.

One night, Dad got drunk—which had become a common occurrence at that point—and he beat up Luca pretty badly. By that point, I was fifteen, but Luca was only six. I took what I had learned from Angel and did what I had to do.

After that, Angel took us all in, and we became his boys.

Angel was gone now, and the Devil took his place.

"I'm not going anywhere." Selena lifted her chin at me.

I'd already grown tired of her impudence.

Reaching over, I did something I had been itching to do. Curling my fingers through her hair, I pulled her head back. She winced and tried to stop me, but it didn't work—it never did.

"Listen up, little dove, as I will only say this once. I own you now. The deal I made with your father means you do what I say. If I tell you to eat a lemon, you don't hesitate. If I tell you to stay naked, you don't put a stitch of clothing on. And if I tell you to get in that house, then you'd better start walking."

I pushed her forward. She stumbled and glanced back. I expected fear to lace her stare, but was surprised when I saw hatred. I knew it well; it was the same look I gave my father the night he died.

23

Despite her anger, she did as I instructed. Once we were inside, I ordered Ricco to take her to the room. He knew what I meant.

I made my way to the kitchen. When I walked into the large, cream-colored kitchen, I saw Elba standing over the sink, eating a peach.

"Don't you have your own food?" I pulled at my tie, removing and tossing it onto the white marble island counter.

"Yeah, but you're the only one who gets Aunt Celia's peaches." My brother wiped at the juice dripping down his chin.

I glanced at the wooden basket that contained my aunt's fruit and noticed several missing. "Just ask her to send you some."

I loved my brother, but he never lost that thieving tendency. If he liked something, he'd take it, and it didn't matter if he got in trouble or not.

"I could, but..." He continued to eat the peach.

My mom's sister, Celia, had moved down to Virginia when she married a farmer. Her husband died about five years ago, and she took over. I tried to pay her for the fresh fruit and vegetables she sent all the time, but she refused every time. She told me family never pays.

Celia knew what I did to my father, yet she still loves me. I asked her once why she would even want to speak to me after that, and she simply told me that I had my mother's smile. That when I smiled, it was as if her sister were smiling from heaven. And once my father was gone, she finally saw my smile again after it had disappeared for so many years. What I did may not have been right, but it was needed.

I didn't believe her because someone like me didn't deserve to be loved. Everyone knows there's no love for the Devil. And that was a role I willingly took on the moment Angel tucked me under his wing.

"But it's more fun to take from other people." Elba grinned.

"Why are you here?" My brother never visited unless there was a reason.

He resented how I handled Dad, but he understood that you stick by family at all costs. With Elba, I had someone to be my eyes and ears. But the moment something bad happened to me, he'd easily move on.

Elba washed his hands in the sink. "One of the Dratshev brothers made an appearance yesterday."

My blood ran cold. I thought I had more time, but it looked like I was wrong. And I was never wrong.

"Where?"

"The Golden Tower."

My jaw tightened. We owned that building. The Dratshev family dared to step foot on the very first property I bought after Angel's death. When I took over.

"They're sending a message," I grumbled.

My brother sighed after he took a handkerchief from his jacket pocket and wiped the last remnants of peach off his face.

"Perhaps, but I have heard nothing from my contacts, so maybe he was lost."

"Which Dratshev brother?"

My brother frowned. "Marko."

He suspected the Dratshev family when it came to Angel's death, but I had a different opinion. They had always wanted our territory and thought once the king was gone, they could take over.

They didn't expect the Devil to appear in his place.

They ran after that because they knew I was after them. But I guess they came back. That was a mistake.

I rubbed my chin, contemplating what it meant when Ricco walked in. "She's in the room."

I nodded. "Thanks, Ricco. Tell Ms. Marta to send something up for her to eat."

Ricco hesitated, which wasn't a good sign.

"What is it?" I raised my brow.

"When I asked if she was hungry, she said she'd rather starve than eat your food. Oh, and when I pointed out the shower, she said she'd rather smell like a rat than use anything this place has to offer. Those were her exact words."

"Ms. Marta?" my brother asked.

"She's the new cook I hired a week ago since Danni disappeared."

It was strange because Danni had been with our family for almost a decade. But then we got word she had left the country and figured something must have happened to her son in Canada. I thought she'd at least tell us she was leaving.

"Then who is this woman in the room, and when can I meet her?" Elba smiled.

I folded my arms. "You won't be meeting her."

Selena was mine. My brothers were not to speak to her or go anywhere near her.

Elba tilted his head. "Now I'm really curious. Why won't you tell me about her?"

Because my brother hated me, he rarely respected my wishes, and only did what he had to for the family. My other brothers—Vitale, Iggy, and Luca—wouldn't even question me.

Elba questioned and fought me at every turn.

"We have bigger problems to focus on. I'm aware of the Dratshev brothers' style. They don't just take or kill; they torture. They will find our weakness and then slowly twist a screw into it until one of us breaks. Marko was just gathering information, just like you do, Elba."

My brother nodded. "I'll tell my contacts to make note when any of the Dratshev brothers appear."

I removed my gold cufflinks and slipped them into my jacket pocket. "Yes. Please tell Iggy he's having dinner with me tonight. I've got to shower as I had a little mishap in a kitchen this morning."

"Which color?" Ricco asked.

I glanced out the large bay window over the sink into the black night. "The tan suit, Ricco."

He nodded and left.

"You're welcome to the dinner, but I suspect you have other plans."

Elba rarely ate with me, but he always wanted in on information. That was his job, to gather info, and he kept the family working. Without him, we would have perished years ago.

I was just the evil son of a bitch who had no heart, so I could easily do the dirty things that kept us all alive.

Elba didn't answer; instead, he just walked away. He thought I was ignorant of who he hung out with, but I was not. He may have had contacts, but so did I.

Now it was time to clean myself off and pay my new guest a visit.

Chapter 4

S elena

    I had to get out of here.

There was no way Domenick would not kill me. He'd use me up for whatever his sick needs required, and then do to me what he did to my landlord.

The room that guy Ricco put me in was an obvious attempt to trick me since it oozed total luxury. He wanted to surround me with opulence so I would relax, and then, when I trusted him, that was when he'd do it. The Devil would take advantage of my naivete and kill me.

The only problem with that was I knew enough not to trust people like him. My mom may have grown up poor, but her family was like his. My dad thought she was different, but he was so wrong. It was in their blood. These crime families were born and raised to be heartless.

I couldn't believe I was taken by Domenick Satriano, the Devil himself. I wasn't some badass woman who could get herself out of sticky situations like in that action flick Camela and I saw on Saturday.

That was a movie, but this was real life... and apparently, I sucked at it.

I walked over to the full length mirror in the short hallway that separated the bedroom from the bathroom and stared at myself. I was a mess. My hair was tangled, and my mascara was running down my face.

Ricco told me to shower, but explaining my opinion of this place to him seemed more important. Now I wanted to clean up, but felt like if I did, then I'd be giving into what the Devil wanted.

Ugh, a hot shower would feel so good right now.

As I was staring at the gold finish of the showerhead, there was a knock at the door. Before I could say a thing, it opened. My eyes darted around the room. Should I hide in the bathroom? Never come out?

I nibbled my lower lip. There was no hiding from the inevitable.

I pushed my shoulders back and prepared for the Devil.

"Hello, miss?" a woman called out.

My eyes widened, and I turned the corner back into the bedroom. A woman with soft gray curls smiled at me. She held a large golden tray, filled with covered dishes and a glass of what looked like milk.

"Where would you like me to put this?"

I folded my arms. "Just take it back. I'm not eating anything this place offers."

She ignored me and glanced around. The woman walked over to a glass coffee table and placed the tray on top.

"There you go. Now you have some nourishing food for whenever you're feeling peckish." She had a faint accent I couldn't place.

The woman was kind, and I felt bad that she had to work for such a man like Mr. Satriano. I wondered if she was here for a debt too.

My eyes slid to the floor. "You really shouldn't have gone to so much trouble."

"No trouble at all, miss." Her gray eyes studied me as if she saw something I couldn't. "You appear quite sad for one so beautiful and young."

She lifted a small black notebook that was on the tray. "I find that it helps me to write how I feel on paper. This isn't Mr. Satriano's idea; this was my idea. I thought, since this is all new to you, it might help to have something private, just for you."

31

Was it that obvious I needed help? My lips thinned. Even she knew I didn't belong here. I should be happy about that. Who would want to look like they fit into a crime family?

I knew the gesture was kind, but I had never felt so alone. The Devil might have been a horrible monster, but he had something I lacked: confidence. And the way the older woman gazed at me, I knew she saw my faults for what they were: weakness.

What I wouldn't give to have Mr. Satriano's strength. Then I wouldn't care that my mom left me, and I certainly wouldn't be stuck in this palatial room awaiting my doom.

"Thank you." She was kind, and I was raised to appreciate that. "Sometimes beauty and youth can be a bad thing. It can mask pain." Then I whispered, "It can attract bad people."

She nodded. "In some cases, yes, but sometimes what appears to be bad can be masking something wonderful behind it." She sighed. "Anyway, I do sometimes wish to be your age once again. I'd do so much differently." Her smile faltered.

There was a pang in my chest. I didn't even know the woman, yet I felt her hurt as if it were my own. From her expression, I could tell she had experienced a loss or hardship, and I understood. No matter how much you pushed the pain away, it always had a habit of bubbling back to the surface in the worst ways.

"But can't control time, now, can we?" She smiled, easily shrugging off her pain.

Wish I had that ability.

She reached down and lifted the lid from one plate. "Bistecca alla Fiorentina. The meat is tender and delicious." She lifted her fingers to her lips and kissed them.

"Then, on the side, I gave you creamy risotto and some asparagus from the garden." She lowered the cover and lifted another cover to display a colorful salad. "And to top it off, I gave you a glass of milk. We have a farm down the road, so it's fresh."

My stomach screamed as everything she showed made my mouth water. I had never experienced food like that before. It was something I suspected only the elite had access to.

"Maybe I'll have a bite…" I couldn't help it. The food was too tempting.

She gave a satisfied grin. "I think that's best. Nothing like a good, hearty meal to help you feel like new."

The woman came over and pulled me in for a hug. It surprised me that she did it at all without knowing me.

But more shocking was my reaction. My eyes burned as I tried to hold back my tears. She felt like the mother I always wanted—kind and willing to comfort me when I needed it most.

She wasn't anything like the mom I had. My mother was distant and made me feel like a burden every chance she could. It hurt when she left, but I wasn't as surprised as Dad. To him, it was a shock, but to me, it felt natural for her to do such a thing.

She pulled away. "I'm Ms. Marta. You let me know if you need anything to eat. I can cook up whatever you'd like. Food binds us all together." Ms. Marta cupped my cheek and then turned away, leaving before I could even respond.

I liked her. Maybe I could survive this knowing I had a friend like Ms. Marta here to help me.

I glanced over at the food, and another thought popped into my head.

Maybe she was sent to get me to let down my defenses? Was she pretending to be nice so I'd confide in her, and then Mr. Satriano would discover what I really thought and use it against me?

I rubbed my brow. Everything was so fucked up.

Taking a deep breath, I reminded myself I was here to help my father. I just had to survive whatever terrible things the Devil had planned for me. Then, when it was all over, I could go back to my father. We could rebuild our lives together, far away from Chicago.

Far away from the Devil's hand.

I inhaled, and the scent of grilled steak caused me to sigh. I told that Ricco guy I wouldn't eat anything, but I lied because I was about to inhale that meat. Lifting a small lid, I saw an individual-sized apple tartlet. I almost cried because, just yesterday, I had learned from my spice book that too much nutmeg was dangerous.

Was that what Domenick wanted? To poison my food?

I frowned as my stomach rumbled.

Sitting on the velvet couch, I lifted the gold steak knife. Suddenly, the bedroom door swung open.

I glanced up to find Mr. Satriano—his hair wet, and he was now wearing a tan suit—standing there, glaring at me. Lowering the steak knife, I hesitated. It was a weapon and the only thing I had to protect myself from the monster in my doorway.

He strolled into the room while loosening his tie and unbuttoning the top button of his white shirt.

He looked around the room and, with his back to me, asked, "Is the room to your liking?"

"No." I stood but held the knife behind my back.

My mind raced at how I would escape once I stabbed him. I was on the second floor, so if I had to, I could jump out the window. The fall would hurt, but at least I'd survive.

With my heart thundering in my ears, I moved toward him.

"That's a shame, as you're going to be in here a long time."

"How long?"

"That's why I'm here... to discuss our upcoming marriage."

My step faltered. Marriage? He still thought I was going to marry him? I only said that to get him away from my father.

"I'm not marrying you. Torture me if you want, make me beg, but I'll never agree to be your bride." I took another step and was close enough that I could lunge and stab him in the back. My palms were sweating, making me grip the smooth golden handle even tighter.

Mr. Satriano turned. His chocolate-brown eyes flared with something as he watched me. Did he know what was behind my back? He was smart, but despite what my mom used to tell me, no one had eyes in the back of their head.

"Yes, to all of that. I will have you beg for me in no time at all, little dove." He closed the distance between us and grabbed my chin.

"I haven't gotten to where I am in life without understanding people. Why they do what they do. If you understand the mind, then you can get someone to do anything you want. And if they don't do what I say, then I take care of them. Whether you're family or not, I will take you out if I have to."

I swallowed. Had he hurt his family before? I had heard rumors that he once killed a relative, but I didn't know if that was true or merely exaggeration.

The way his eyes raked over my mouth caused my pussy to dampen. I hated that my body reacted to him, but I knew one thing for certain: I'd never have sex with him.

"And you, little dove, will beg for my cock, and that won't take long at all." He smirked.

He let go of my chin and took off his jacket. Now was my chance. While he was turning to throw his jacket onto the pale pink bedspread, I lifted my arm. My hand shook. I had never stabbed someone before. Sure, I had a few fights in high school with some bitches who thought they were tough, but nothing was used that could cause death.

I held my breath and, with all my strength, lowered my hand toward his shoulder, by his neck. He quickly turned and grabbed my wrist before I could stab him.

The man was fast.

His fingers tightened, causing me to lose my grip. The golden knife fell to the hardwood floor with a *clank*.

His nostrils flared, but there was a smile on his lips. "Oh, little dove... you shouldn't have done that. You're feisty, but not nearly quick enough." He kicked the knife across the room toward the door.

"Fuck you," I gritted through my teeth and tried to hit him with my free hand, but again, he stopped me before I could.

"A little too feisty."

He moved around me, only letting go of one of my wrists for a second before grabbing it again, and pinned my hands behind my back.

His grip was so tight that it caused my chest to jut out. The Devil pushed me forward until my legs hit the foot of the bed.

Then he bent me over. I closed my eyes because I knew what he was about to do. How could I have been so stupid to believe I could kill the Devil?

The roughest gangsters and cops couldn't take him down, yet I thought I could?

He yanked the top of my leggings down, grabbing my undies too. It wasn't long before my ass was exposed. I tried to squirm and pull out of his hold, but he was too strong for me.

"It's time to teach you a lesson. Never try to fuck with me." He punctuated his point with his hand slapping my ass, and it wasn't gentle. He spanked me like I was a child.

I held back a cry from the flash of pain, but after a few seconds, that throbbing pain deepened. It morphed into pleasure that tingled between my thighs.

My eyes widened. It was such a surprise that I let out a moan.

"What was that, little dove?" He spanked me again. "You want more?"

I licked my lips, trying to muffle my cries as my pussy throbbed. But the second slap was different. He was more attentive, rubbing his hand over my tender flesh.

"Do you want one more, or have you learned your lesson?"

I nibbled on my lower lip. This was humiliating, and I wanted it to end. How could my body betray me like that?

But what came out of my mouth surprised me.

"One more, please."

Chapter 5

D omenick

It was the *please* that did it for me. My cock had throbbed the moment I saw her plump, smooth and thick ass. Thoughts of how it would shake as I fucked her made my mouth water.

But when she begged me to spank her again, that made my cock rock-hard.

I gave her a swift slap, and the ripples moved across her ass cheeks as the delicious sound of her moan filled the room.

The finest silk surrounded us, hand-carved furniture from Italy, and ancient vases filled with freshly picked flowers, but it could all burn into ash because Selena's body was the only thing I coveted. I had never been with a woman who responded to my touch like Selena had. I had never been with one who caused me to react so quickly.

I had planned to just spank her, but my curiosity caused my plans to change. Slipping my fingers between her thighs, I felt her wetness.

"Already soaked." She gasped as I slid a finger inside her.

Moving my hand, I pumped my finger in and out before I slid another finger over her clit. Taking a risk, I let go of her hands I had pinned against her back, and she didn't move away.

Selena wanted my touch. She had begged for it.

"Do you get this wet for every guy, or is it just me?"

"Fuck you," she moaned and pushed back against my hand as her hips gyrated.

Fuck, she was gorgeous. I was walking a tightrope with Selena, and I had to be careful I never fell.

"Not yet, little dove."

"Stop calling me that." She placed her hands on the bedspread, and her fingers curled into the pale pink silk.

I slid my hand from between her thighs and stepped away. Her bare ass was on display for me, stained pink from my touch.

Making my way over to the bathroom sink, I washed my hands. I had wanted to lick my fingers clean, but I knew it was too soon. Selena was already invading my brain far more than she should have, so it was best to wash away any further temptations.

When I turned back, she was pulling up her leggings.

Her cheeks were flushed, and she kept her gaze downcast. I wanted to push her to her knees and make her suck me off for how she spoke to me.

I slid my hand over my hard cock, trying to push it down, but with her in the room, there was no hope. "Do you want your father to die?" I shoved my hands in the pockets of my slacks and tilted my head.

Her head popped up, eyes widened. "No! Please, don't kill him."

"I don't kill people."

An adorable wrinkle appeared in the middle of her brow. "But my landlord, Mr. Banks, you—"

"Karma."

She folded her arms over her chest. "You're telling me that *karma* beheaded him?"

The corner of my mouth curled. It was going to be tough curing her of that smart mouth, but I was going to have fun doing it.

"Things happen to people who deserve them. I don't kill them; I just give them what they deserve. Mr. Banks wasn't a good guy, so karma came along and robbed him of his head." I shrugged.

"How do you know he wasn't a good guy?" Her eyes narrowed.

She was smart. I liked that about her. Most people never questioned me, but Selena wasn't scared of how I'd react. She might have had a mouth on her, but I already learned I enjoyed what came out of it.

"I have people who monitor things for me. They had seen what he was doing. What he did to you."

All the pretty color in her cheeks drained. Selena opened her mouth to speak but said nothing.

"And *that*, I don't tolerate. Especially when someone messes with my things."

"Wh... what thing of yours did he mess with?"

I walked over to her and pushed her arms until they were hanging at her side. Her skin was soft as silk, and I had an intense need to touch it. I slid my fingers up her neck until my thumb smoothed across her cheek, where the color was warming her skin once again.

"My little dove."

That wrinkle in her brow appeared again. "*Me?* But that happened before you made a deal with my dad."

A soft chuckle escaped my lips. "You think I made a deal? I didn't. I told you and your father that you had a say, but I lied. This, little dove," I gestured between us, "was my plan all along."

Her green eyes grew, and she stepped back. "What? This was all a trap? To marry me?"

"You have me mistaken for my brother Elba. He's the hunter, laying traps. I, on the other hand, just take. I decided I wanted you and took you, simple as that. Now, here you are."

Her eyes moved around the room wildly. I knew what she was about to do and wasn't looking forward to this moment, but I had to tell her. "You don't seem to realize, little dove, that life is a game. It's tough and sometimes very tricky, but if you play it right, then the rewards are endless."

That was when she ran. Instead of trying to bolt past me, she ran with all her strength straight into me. It surprised me, but then again, Selena was full of surprises.

But if her aim was to knock me over, she had no chance. I was bigger and much stronger than her.

I grabbed her arm and pulled her to me. Her hot breath fluttered across my neck as I gently pushed some of her locks out of her face and tucked them behind her ear. "Where do you think you're going?"

"Away from you," she bit out. "Everyone calls you the Devil, but I think they're wrong. You're just an insane monster."

I knew what people called me, and I relished it. It meant people were scared me. I'd rather be feared than allow anyone to attempt to hurt me.

"Perhaps. But I will warn you, little dove, you either learn to play the game, or you'll lose. And trust me when I say you really don't want to lose." I let her go and went to grab my jacket off the bed.

"Maybe I do want to lose. You don't know me like you think you do."

My jaw clenched. It was time to end her nonsense.

I pivoted and twisted her hair in my hand, pulling her head back. "I don't know you, huh? So, if I shove my hand into your pussy again, it won't be wet? Because I'm guessing it will."

I yanked at her hair until she walked to the bed, then I bent her over. Shoving her head down, I bent over next to Selena, facing her. "Tell me to stop. Tell me you don't want this." I took my free hand and ripped down her leggings and panties.

She whimpered but didn't open her mouth. Not a single, breathless word escaped her lips. If I had whipped out my cock, I bet she would have begged me to fill her.

I wasn't gentle this time. My hand reached between her thighs and roughly shoved several fingers into her pussy. Her eyes widened.

"Soaking. Just as I thought." I removed my hand and slapped her ass before pushing my fingers back into her pussy.

She wiggled her ass, and that was it. I lost control.

"Tell me to stop," I growled.

She never did.

I finger-fucked her, and it wasn't long before she cried out my name.

Not Mr. Satriano... not the Devil.

She said *Domenick.*

My other hand squeezed her ass cheek, and I took a shaky breath before slipping my hand out from inside her. I stood, grabbed my jacket, and left the room.

Standing on the other side of her door, I stared at the large floral oil painting that hung directly across from me. My heart beat wildly as I focused on one pink petal as it slipped from the flower and fell toward the dark table below.

Swallowing, I pushed my shoulders back. That shouldn't have happened. No one had ever made me lose it like that. It was as if Selena had reached deep inside me and allowed her fingers to flutter across my heart.

My heart died years ago. I killed it myself when I ended my father. It was better that way. Getting attached to people, especially women, could cause problems. It was a weakness, and something the Dratshev family could easily take advantage of.

My brothers, especially Vitale, enjoyed the ladies a little too much, which put them at risk. I had to help Vitale more times than I liked. I shipped him off to Italy to stay with family, but from what I heard, it hadn't helped.

I fucked women whenever I wanted, but that it. It was transactional. They'd get a sumptuous meal, some fine wine, and whatever they wished for, which was usually jewelry.

Then, in the morning, Ms. Marta would make them an exquisite breakfast and send them on their way. No one ever complained.

But I was growing older. Now, at almost forty, I knew it was time to think about having children. We were a family, and, therefore, it had to grow.

Selena was beautiful and perfect. She cared for her father like any good daughter would, so I knew she had that motherly instinct.

"There you are." Iggy gave me his typical big toothy grin.

Iggy was the second-youngest brother. He was the one who made the tough decisions, like who should be taken out. Most people called him Ice because that was how cold he was.

By outside appearances, he seemed like a fun-loving guy who always had a smile on his face, but it was all for show. To fool people into believing that he liked them, and they were safe. They weren't.

Even I wasn't safe from Iggy. I knew that, but most others never did.

While Dad beat Luca and left physical scars on his body, what he did to Iggy was much worse. My father left scars on Iggy too, but they were the kind the naked eye could never find. He mentally fucked with Iggy.

I slipped on my jacket and straightened my tie. It was best if Iggy knew nothing about Selena.

Iggy's eyes slid to Selena's door but quickly refocused on me. If I had blinked, I wouldn't have noticed. But I knew to remain vigilant whenever Iggy was around.

"I'm glad you could make it for dinner." I reached over and slapped him on his shoulder.

Iggy was slightly shorter than me, but he made up for height with muscle. He gave no one a reason to question him. All he had to do was face them, and they'd back down.

"Who is she?"

My nostrils flared. "Who is who?"

Iggy stood and glared at my hand until I removed it from his shoulder.

I ran my fingers through my hair. There wasn't a person on Earth I was afraid of, except for Izzy. The only reason he didn't run the family was because he enjoyed being in the background. All the responsibilities that came with running our family weren't his thing.

"The woman you have staying in the room."

I didn't want Iggy to know, but he was too smart for me.

"Just some girl I'm fooling around with. No one special." I shrugged.

Chapter 6

S elena

I stood there, naked, my hair slightly damp from the shower I had taken. I studied my body. How could it betray me like that?

My palm flattened over my stomach, then slid around until I was touching where the Devil had marked me. There was no bruise from what he had done to me two days ago, but he imprinted the memory, never to be removed. I was thankful he left me alone yesterday. It gave me time to think up ways to get out of here.

I nibbled on my lips and thought about everything that had happened.

The strength of Domenick's hand on my skin sent shock-waves through my body, as if I was being electrocuted. His grip was like a vise, punishing me for the smallest infraction. I became breathless when his fingers plunged deep inside me, sending ripples of pleasure and pain coursing through me with each thrust.

It sickened me how I wanted more. What sort of person craved a monster's touch?

Domenick Satriano was a stranger to me. All I knew about him was what I had been told, and it wasn't good. But the man who laid his hands on me two days ago... that man was an addiction. I wanted more, even if it left me weak and wanting. And that was why I had to leave.

I shook my head as I picked up the pile of clothes I had discarded and wondered if I should put them back on. Or maybe I would see what the Devil had picked out for me.

I went to put my clothes on but then saw how dirty they were. As much as I avoided it, I was going to have to wear the clothes Domenick had provided.

After tossing my clothes in a wicker basket in the corner, I put the hair dryer back in the drawer before I left the bathroom. Staring at the opulent king-sized bed, I opened the closet Ricco had pointed out when I first arrived. I had refused to even look inside yesterday, but now I had no choice.

I pulled open the closet's ornately carved dark wood door with the crystal doorknob. My head shot back at what I saw. It was another room, almost as big as the bedroom.

As I walked inside, my eyes savored an array of colors and textures that filled the room, from soft cottons to shiny silks and satins. Colorful blouses, trousers, skirts, and dresses hung from poles along the walls, each a unique work of art. In the middle of each wall was a tall bookshelf, stuffed with shoes of every style, from sexy stilettos to comfy sandals. Above that was a shelf lined with purses of all colors and shapes.

I reached for a pale pink blouse and slipped it on. The fabric was silky and luxurious against my skin, like a gentle caress. The hem just brushed my upper thighs as I put it on, enveloping me in its comfortable embrace.

I twirled around and bumped into a marble island. It was like something I would find in a fancy kitchen, but it was in the middle of a closet. When I walked around it, I saw small dark wood drawers on either side.

There was a hand mirror on top of the island—made of gold, of course. It seemed everything in this home was touched by gold. Did Domenick have the golden touch like the fairy tale my dad read to me when I was young?

I suspected it was the opposite. Instead of making everything golden, the Devil's touch caused misery and ruined people's lives.

Opening one of the small drawers, I gasped. My hand shook as I reached for the necklace. It was made of gold but looked like the most delicate floss with a golden heart dangling from the end.

I had worn nothing so beautiful before. Any jewelry I wore was cheap and turned my skin green or was made of plastic. This necklace even felt different.

I held it up to my neck and wondered what it would look like on me.

"What's stopping you?" I heard a deep voice from behind.

I gasped and dropped the necklace onto the marble counter.

He stood there in a fitted white button-up shirt and dark pants. And I noticed something I hadn't before. The flecks of gold that adorned him. The golden belt buckle, a gold watch that twinkled as he lifted his hand and scratched his dark beard.

"Why gold?"

"It's just a necklace. A lot of them come in gold, so I bought it."

I noticed his usual dark, toe-curling stare was gone. His eyes moved around the room like a bee with no flower to land on.

"Not the necklace. I meant this..." I waved my arms around. "Your home. There isn't a room I've been in where gold hasn't touched it."

"I like gold."

He finally lifted his eyes and stared. It was just a look, but it told me so much. The main thing it told me was not to ask questions.

I swallowed and was about to poke the beehive when thoughts of my father popped into my head. Rolling my lips over my teeth, I kept my mouth shut.

51

If his love of gold was a touchy subject for him, then so be it.

"It's not my necklace." I lifted the jewelry to put it back.

"It is now. Put it on."

He didn't wait for me to respond. Domenick came over and plucked the necklace from my hand. He stepped behind me and placed the delicate piece around my neck.

His fingers brushed my collarbone, and gooseflesh broke out over my skin. He pushed my hair over my shoulder and leaned close. His hot breath fluttered down my neck as he whispered, "Whatever you want, I'll give you. You will need nothing I can't provide, little dove."

My fingers shook as I reached up to touch the golden heart, feeling my heart beat wildly in my chest as my fingers brushed my skin.

The necklace was secured, but he didn't move. For a moment, I thought he would lean closer and kiss my neck. My mind was in a battle with my heart.

My chest rapidly moved up and down as the war raged inside me. I tilted my head, but he stepped back, his hands lifting away from me, leaving my skin feeling icy where his hands once lay.

I should have been happy he was walking away, but my chest ached for him to turn back. I closed my eyes and took a breath.

Good. He should leave. Then my thoughts would clear. I could focus on coming up with a plan to get myself out of here and to make sure my dad was okay.

When Domenick got to the door, he closed it. He wasn't leaving at all. What did he want to do to me in the closet? Was he going to bend me over the marble island and spank me again?

My pussy throbbed at the thought, and I swallowed.

"Come here." He reached out his hand, and I took it.

My nipples hardened when I saw our reflection in the full-length mirror that hung on the door. I hated to admit it, but there was a thrill at seeing him pull me beside him. As if he was protecting me from invisible danger.

He moved behind me and lifted my hair that had fallen across my chest. The necklace sparkled around my neck.

"See? It's beautiful on you. I made everything here for you."

That made little sense... I just arrived yesterday.

"These clothes will fit me?"

"Yes." His hand slid around my neck, tilting my chin up. "I know you want to fight me, little dove. You want to run, but that would be unwise."

His hand slid down my neck until he was cupping my breast. Heat ignited between my thighs as he drifted his thumb over the silk that covered my nipple.

"You're mine now. And when you're mine, I'll give you nothing but the best. And I won't let anyone hurt you or your father. Family always takes care of family, you understand?"

I could barely focus on his words with how he was pinching my nipple. I reached up to touch his hand, but he slapped my arm away.

"I'm not your family," I said before releasing a moan.

Not yet.

My hands fisted at my side since he wouldn't let me touch him.

"The moment I touched you, you became family to me."

My pussy was ready to burst with the way he was fondling me. It must have been obvious because the way he watched me in the mirror was so dark, I briefly wondered if he wanted to fuck me or kill me.

He held me there, my back pressed against his front, roughly playing me like a guitar. I couldn't take it anymore, so I tried to reach between my thighs to relieve the pressure.

"Don't touch yourself."

He wanted me to beg for him, but I refused to do it. I made a mistake yesterday—one I would never repeat.

"Only I will give you orgasms, you understand?"

That must have been his thing—to make women climax. I felt his hard cock dig into my back, so it wasn't as if he was immune to what was happening between us. I was relieved he wasn't using it, since it felt enormous.

I had fooled around with guys before, but I was a virgin, and I feared his enormous cock might break me.

"I want to come," I whimpered.

The corner of his mouth twitched. "That's all I needed to hear."

I let out a breath of relief as I readied myself for more. But it never happened. He let go of me and stepped away. I stumbled backward until I was leaning on the island. When I glanced up at Domenick, he was straightening his tie.

"Tomorrow, at this time, I will be taking you to lunch. Make sure to be ready. Wear the outfit I picked out for you in the cabinet." He pointed to the long, thin cabinet door that was next to the shoe shelves on the opposite side of the closet.

Then he opened the door to the closet and left.

I stood there, my body still throbbing from his touch, wondering what had just happened. From the moment Domenick Satriano entered my life, he had twisted and turned me so much that I could barely stand whenever I was near him.

Chapter 7

D omenick

I watched a gorgeous woman step out of the black Maserati Quattroporte with a grace that suggested she knew no other way to be. Her beauty was undeniable, with her dark sunglasses and long, chocolate hair blowing in the wind. Selena's red lips thinned when she saw me waiting, and her blue flower-print skirt swayed in the warm breeze.

I could hear the faint hum of the car as it idled and the soft rustle of her skirt as it danced in the wind. Her white silk blouse fluttered as she ascended the stairs. I stepped aside when she got to the top. A fragrant mix of summer flowers wafted through the air as I waved her inside.

"I thought you said we were going to lunch? Where is the restaurant? Rome?" She let out a hard chuckle.

"No, little dove." I nodded to the air hostess to take Selena to her leather seat. "It's in Florence."

She removed her sunglasses and stared at me as I sat directly across from her. "You rented a private jet to take me to lunch in Florence, Italy?"

Leaning back, I couldn't help but smile. It had been so long since someone amused me as much as Selena.

"No, I rent nothing. I *own*."

Her brows shot up, and an adorable tiny wrinkle appeared between them. "You own this plane? What don't you own?"

I was about to answer her before she held up her hand. "Don't answer that."

I leaned back against the soft, rich creamy leather of the chair, my gaze fixed on Selena. Her eyes darted around the interior of the jet, taking in its plushness and luxury. The rich fabrics of the seats and walls glimmered in the light, and a faint smell of newness still lingered in the air.

"You know," she said, "I'm not very good with surprises. I like to know what I'm getting into."

"That might be a problem with what I do. You're going to have to get used to surprises with me."

She sat there quietly as she studied me.

"You look lovely."

The stylist I hired for Selena did a wonderful job. Those rags she wore when I first met her were terrible. She dressed like a girl,

57

but she was a woman, and the clothes she wore now reflected that.

"It's a little old-fashioned for my taste." She plucked at the blouse sleeve.

"Classic."

"What?"

"It's a classic style; something that is timeless. If you want to command attention, then always wear something that will never go out of fashion."

She pursed her lips and glanced out the airplane window. "It's not like I have a choice," she mumbled, but I heard.

I was getting a sense of her reactions, and I knew something was brewing in her head. Observing people was part of my job—it was what kept me and my family alive.

Clearing her throat, she shook off whatever was distracting her. "I don't have a passport." She kept looking out the window.

"That's not a problem."

"It is a problem if you expect them to let me into the country."

"It has all been taken care of."

The plane moved down the runway, and I knew it would be in the air in no time. Selena's fingers dug into the armrests.

"Have you ever flown before?"

She shook her head, and when she finally glanced over at me, I saw the fear in her eyes. I didn't like that look on her.

"Come here." I waved her over.

She pressed back into her seat.

"Don't be childish. Nothing bad will happen. Come here, Selena."

She glanced around the cabin. "Is it safe for me to stand?"

"We haven't taken off yet, and you're only taking two steps over to me." I lifted my hand to help her across.

She let out a sigh and stood. Once she was in front of me, I grabbed her hips, and she let out a yelp as I pulled her down onto my lap.

"I'm not a child."

I smirked. I guess she didn't like my childish comment about her. I made a mental note that she wanted respect and to be treated with dignity. That was an excellent trait and something I could use to my advantage.

I wrapped my arms around her and noticed she didn't push me away. In fact, she slid her hands into my arms and held me tight.

Right at that moment, the plane took off.

"Oh god," she whispered.

I lifted my hand to the back of her neck and massaged. If the stylist hadn't wrapped her hair up in a French twist, I would massage her scalp, but I didn't want to mess with what the stylist had done.

Her hips moved, causing my cock to stir. When I inhaled, I noticed a distinct scent on her. Floral. Jasmine. It was perfect for Selena.

My fingers slid from around her waist and over her thighs. I had spent years building up my defenses. I was like a rock, but Selena embedded the tiniest crack.

The plane dipped as it flew higher in the air, and that movement snapped me back to myself. "It's time to head back to your seat, little dove."

She didn't immediately get up, which surprised me. When I had my fingers in her pussy several days ago, she didn't stop me, nor yesterday when I was fondling her tits. But that was different. Any woman, if aroused enough, would melt to my touch.

This time, I wasn't doing anything to her. So why was she hesitating?

After a few more moments, she stood and returned to her seat.

Once we reached cruising altitude, the stewardess brought out drinks—whiskey for me and wine for Selena.

"I don't drink. And besides, I'm not twenty-one." Selena frowned at the red liquid in the wineglass on the small wooden-topped table in front of her.

I chuckled. "We're going to Italy. To them, a twenty-year-old woman is old enough to drink wine or anything else she likes."

"I like pop."

Now it was my turn to frown. "That is just sugar water with bubbles."

She folded her arms. "That's what I like."

Then Selena made a mistake: she bit down on her bottom lip. She was playing with me. These little fights with her were just a game… a game that she controlled.

But not anymore.

I put down my whiskey and plucked up her wineglass. After unbuckling my seatbelt, I rose and went over to her. "Open your mouth."

She jerked her head back. "You can't be serious?"

"Little dove, don't test me. Now, open your mouth."

Her lips thinned as she glared up at me. It was amusing that she thought she could win the tug-of-war game she had created.

But I always got what I wanted.

I reached down with my free hand and slid my finger across her cheek. Her gaze tried to remain on my face, but she was unsure what I would do next.

She didn't know me the way I knew her.

Her eyes dipped to my hand and watched as I moved down her neck and over her shoulder. My fingers caressed her soft skin as I moved down her arm. As I bent over, my breath blew across her neck.

Her chest moved up at down, faster and faster. Her lips softened, and all I wanted to do was nibble on them. Despite the distraction, I shook it off and kept moving my hand down until I was lifting the hem of her skirt.

"Here? Where people can see?" Selena's words were breathless.

"I can do what I want on my plane."

My fingers found the heat of her apex. She was wet. When she relaxed her thighs, opening them for me, I knew I had her.

Her mouth sagged open as my finger brushed over her lace-covered clit. With my other hand, I lifted the glass to her lips and gave her a small taste.

Her eyes widened, and she let out a moan.

"Now was that so hard?" I straightened and went back to my seat.

Fire ignited behind her eyes as she glared at me, and I realized I was attracted to that heat. There was something about Selena I wasn't expecting.

I shifted in my seat and tried to think about something else. I couldn't let myself get distracted—not with something so important at stake. I watched her sit there, her chin lifted and her back straightened, and a look on her face that was purely venomous.

I didn't know what made me want to laugh, but it did.

"I'm just some funny little toy to you, aren't I? Congratulations, Domenick, you have so much money and power that you can buy brides and force them to drink wine. That must make you so happy at night in your silk-covered bed," she sneered.

"Get down on your knees."

"What?" Her head jerked back.

She enjoyed fucking around so much. Fine. There was a fun game I was creating just for her.

"I said, get down on your knees, Selena."

She frowned as her eyes danced around the cabin. After a moment, she fell to her knees and looked up at me.

I unzipped my trousers and pulled out my cock. It had been hard since she first stepped on the plane, but I was a man who could control myself. Unfortunately, she was a woman who couldn't control her mouth.

"Now suck my cock."

"You can't be serious."

A smile took over my face. She was trying to make me seem like I was taking advantage of her, and she would not get away with that.

Regardless of the fact we were on a plane, I gripped my cock. Selena's eyes widened as I fisted my cock and started stroking it.

I closed my eyes when the precum dripped onto my hands. It was hard to hold myself in. "You wanted to play, so I'm just returning the favor. Now open those lips and suck me off."

Her mouth dropped to the floor, but Selena didn't move.

Suddenly, her smart mouth had nothing to say. I reached down and gripped her hair. "You're going to suck my cock, and you're going to fucking enjoy it. Understand?"

She nodded and leaned forward.

"Look at me before you do anything."

Her eyes lifted to mine.

"Open your mouth and close your lips over the head. Suck. Understand?"

She nodded.

"Good girl." Her head eased toward me, and she took the tip of my cock into her mouth. I groaned as her tongue swirled over my sensitive skin. In and out. Over and over. She moved up and down, soft and slow. Her hand reached up and grabbed the base, pumping slowly as she followed the rhythm of her mouth over my cock.

God, she's fucking incredible.

I closed my eyes and let out a groan. Little by little, Selena was pushing my buttons. It was indescribable. The way she took me in. The way she explored me. It was the most erotically charged experience I had ever faced.

Selena's lips moved up and down, sucking lightly. She swirled her tongue and devoured my cock.

It was a perfect blowjob.

"Fuck." I closed my eyes as she did it again.

She was a virgin, young and soft. She was perfect. She was beautiful.

I gripped her hair in my hand, no longer caring that I was ruining what the stylist had done, as I slammed my cock deeper into her mouth. She gagged a little, but I would not stop. I wanted to teach her a lesson.

I dug my finger into her skin, and her eyes danced up to mine.

"You're not in charge here, Selena. Your mouth will do what I say, and your body will do what I want."

I pulled my cock out of her mouth. She glared up at me as she sat back on her heels. "Who says I don't want to do this?"

I was surprised, but I didn't let it show. Instead, I leaned back and let her finish.

Her tongue darted out of her swollen lips, and she reached for my cock. Her tongue flicked over the tip. When she sucked me inside her hot mouth, I nearly came.

"That's it, little dove. Take it." I cupped her cheeks and jerked her back up so she would go faster.

Her mouth moved faster, and her hand followed along. Before I could stop myself, I was thrusting in and out of her hot mouth. Each time my cock slid in and out of her mouth, I grunted. "Fuck. I'm going to cum. You fucking swallow, or I'll never let you come again."

Her eyes widened, but she kept her lips closed around the head.

My head fell back as I exploded into her mouth.

I came harder and longer than I ever had before. When I opened my eyes, I found Selena was watching me. Her cheeks were flushed, and her eyes were wide.

"Clean me off." I pushed her head back, and she lapped at my cock. When she was done, she sat back.

I grabbed her face and pulled it up. "Did you like that, Selena?"

Her eyes were still wide when she mumbled, "I've never done that before."

It didn't seem like her first time with the way she fucked me with her mouth.

"And it won't be your last time, either."

Chapter 8

S elena

    The hotel room was beautiful. As I had learned in the past four days with Domenick, everything around him was exquisite and usually priceless.

But that was all a façade. Underneath it all was dirty, corrupt, and, with him, hard as stone.

I stood in the center of the room, taking in the lavish surroundings. The delicate chandelier above my head cast a warm glow around the room, illuminating every corner. My gaze swept over the plush silk bedding, the intricate art on the walls, and the expensive furniture. The impeccable white lilies in the crystal vase on the table emitted an intoxicating scent, and I almost smiled.

It was all so beautiful, so perfect, but I knew better than to let my guard down. Even now, I looked for a way to escape.

As I turned to face Domenick, I couldn't help but feel a twinge of fear in my chest. He was an enigma, a mystery that I wondered would ever be solved. Beneath the designer suits and chiseled jaw, there was a darkness he wore like armor. It was intoxicating and dangerous, drawing me in like a moth to a flame.

I gasped at the realization.

I was surprised how much I loved what he made me do on the plane. I nibbled on my lower lip, wondering when he might let me do that again.

I shook my head. What was happening to me?

I wasn't here to fall for his twisted idea of a date. I had to get away from him, figure out a way to leave and save my father. I wouldn't let him distract me from it. Fancy clothes and private jets to Italy might work on the women he usually kept, but not me.

I took a deep breath and stepped closer, my gaze locked on his. "So, why are we here?"

"I am here to meet with my brother, Vitale."

That was different. He wanted me to meet his brother. I knew little about Vitale, but perhaps I could get him to help me escape.

I nibbled my lower lip. "Is that where we're going to lunch?"

Something sinister crossed his eyes. "You'll be dining in the hotel restaurant alone. I was going to join you, but I really need to speak to my brother."

Domenick walked over to me and grabbed my chin. His touch was firm but not painful. "You'll be safe," he said, his voice low and commanding. His thumb slid over my bottom lip, and electricity ran down my spine.

The lunch date was a lie. I knew why I was here, even if he didn't tell me—to make sure I didn't escape. I tried to pull away from him, but his grip was too strong. I felt the heat from his breath on my face as he leaned in closer.

"Remember, you are here to pay for your father's debt. To do what I say." His eyes narrowed. "But if you rather I kill him, then—"

I swallowed hard, feeling the tension building in the room. I had to play along with his madness, at least until I could escape.

"No. I will marry you," I cut him off, my voice barely above a whisper.

I had to lie until I could figure a way out. Domenick released me, and I stumbled back a few steps, gasping for breath.

"Good." He turned and walked toward the door. "I'll send someone to take you to the restaurant."

With that, he left the room, and I was alone for the first time since I set foot in Italy.

I looked around, trying to find a way out that wasn't through the hotel room door. But there was only a terrace with a beautiful view of the Arno River. There was no way I'd jump into that water. I might have been desperate, but I was not desperate enough to take that leap of death.

Sighing, I went back into the room and pulled the notebook Ms. Marta gave me from my bag. Jotting down my thoughts and possible plan for escape, I heard a faint sound from behind me. I turned and saw a small, intricate door that I hadn't noticed before. It was barely visible, camouflaged by the ornate wallpaper. My heart leaped with hope. *Maybe this is my way out.*

I tucked the notebook back into my bag and approached the door. Slowly, I tried twisting the handle, but it was locked.

I looked around frantically, hoping to find a key or something to help me open the door. Then I spotted it—a small keyhole on the door, barely visible in the dim light. I looked around and found nothing.

Ugh, there had to be something in the room.

I ran into the beautifully appointed marble bathroom and pulled out a dark wooden drawer under the counter. My eyes widened in delight.

Jackpot.

I found every hair accessory a woman would need... even bobby pins.

I went back to the tiny door and jiggled the bobby pin around for a few seconds in the keyhole, and suddenly, the lock clicked open. My heart raced as I pushed the door open and stepped into the darkness beyond.

The room was small, and it smelled musty and unused. But there was a bigger door on the far wall, and I raced over to unlock it.

Stepping through the door, darkness surrounded me. Pushing my shoulders back, I took a step, and my foot hit something hard, followed by a clatter.

My heart thundered in my chest as I held my breath, waiting to find out if someone had heard me. When no one came, I reached for the wall and found a switch. When I flipped it up, the lights came on.

I was in a utility closet. And best of all, there was another door in front of me, and I knew it had to lead to a hallway and to freedom.

I took one last look around the closet, leaving no trace of my presence. I couldn't risk Domenick finding out how I escaped. Once I was sure everything was in place, I turned and stepped forward, my hand reaching for the doorknob.

But before I could grab it, the door flung open, and a man stood before me, his eyes wide with shock. "What are you doing here?" he demanded, his voice stern.

"I, uh… I was just looking for the bathroom," I said, trying to keep my voice steady.

The man raised an eyebrow, and I knew he didn't believe me. "Well, you won't find it here," he said, rubbing his chin and leaning against the doorway.

A nervous giggle bubbled up my throat. "I guess not."

He wouldn't move.

"You lost?"

I was so nervous before, I hadn't realized this guy had an American accent.

Who was he? Did he know Domenick?

"Sort of... Just trying to get home."

His dark brown eyes slid down my body. The muscles around them tensed as he inspected me from head to toe. Even with his chiseled good looks, I felt a chill creep up my spine. He wasn't lusting after me; this man was deciding, and I feared what it meant for me.

"Maybe I could help with that." He took a step back and waved for me to step out into the hallway.

I did and noticed the stairs at the end of the hall.

"I wouldn't run if I were you."

He must have noticed me staring.

I swallowed and tried to smile. "Where would I run to? I'm in Italy."

That was when my own words hit me. Where would I run to? I didn't speak Italian. I could speak Spanish, but how far would that get me?

Fuck. I'm trapped.

"I need to find my room." I wrapped my hands around my torso, trying to ward off a sudden chill.

"I thought you wanted to get home?"

I narrowed my eyes at him. "Why do you care so much?"

If Domenick found out this guy was fucking with me, he'd kill him. Sure, I wanted to get away from Domenick, but I didn't want to run into the arms of another psycho to do it.

"You interest me." He shrugged.

I knew it. Total psycho.

Stepping to the side, I pointed down the hall. "I'm going to find my room now." Turning my back to him, I picked up my pace, moving down the hall.

"Alright, Selena. I'm sure we'll meet again."

I came to a stop. Wait... He knew my name?

"Who are you?" I turned back to watch him come toward me.

"I'm Elba. Domenick's brother."

"I thought he was here to visit Vitale?"

He sucked in a breath through his teeth. "That's the thing. Domenick is here to visit Vitale, but I'm here to visit you."

My heart sank. I had barely escaped Domenick's grasp, only to find myself in the clutches of another man. And not just any man, but Domenick's brother. What had I gotten myself into?

Elba stepped closer to me, his eyes darkening. "You don't have to be afraid, Selena. I won't hurt you."

I tried to step away, but the wall was at my back. "What do you want from me?"

He leaned in, his breath hot on my neck. "I want to help you escape. You don't belong here."

I didn't know what to believe. Was this some kind of twisted game they were playing with me? Or was Elba really trying to help me?

"Why would you help me?"

Elba's lips curved into a sly smile that reminded me of Domenick. "Let's just say I have my reasons."

I didn't like the sound of that. But then again, I didn't like the idea of marrying Domenick, either.

"Can you get me back to Chicago?"

"Yes, but you have to—"

"Elba."

I sucked in a breath at the sound of Domenick's voice shouting his brother's name.

Elba turned and smiled. "Domenick, so nice to see you here."

My heart practically stopped beating in my chest as I watched Domenick make his way down the hallway toward us. His eyes were locked on me, and I couldn't help but feel a sense of dread wash over me.

What is he going to do to me?

"What are you doing here, Elba? Last I checked, you were back in Chicago," Domenick growled, his eyes flickering between his brother and me.

"I decided to come visit Vitale," Elba replied casually, his arms crossed over his chest.

Domenick didn't look convinced. "And what about her?" He jerked his head in my direction and shoved his finger into his brother's chest.

The two men stood in front of me. Both were tall—though Domenick was a little taller than his brother—both were muscular, and both looked like they could break me with their bare hands.

Elba shrugged. "She was lost. I was trying to help her get back to her room."

Domenick's eyes narrowed at his brother, and for a moment, I thought he was going to launch himself at Elba. But he turned his attention back to me. "What are you doing out of the room? You were to wait for someone to come get you. Did you think it was Elba?"

I could make the excuse that I thought his brother was to take me to the hotel restaurant, but Elba said he'd help me. I couldn't lie and put the blame on him.

I shook my head. "I tried to leave."

Domenick grabbed my arm and yanked me to a door without a word.

Once we were inside, I turned to face him. "You can't keep me locked up like a prisoner."

He didn't respond. Instead, Domenick removed his jacket and tossed it onto a leather chair close by. He uncuffed his sleeves and rolled them up.

My heart pounded in my chest, and my nipples hardened. He was about to punish me.

Chapter 9

D omenick

Selena stood at the center of the room; her French twist had long since fallen, and her tangled hair radiated around her like a wild halo. Her chest heaved with deep breaths, and her body shook with a frightening intensity. Every inch of her was alive with an undeniable energy—the kind that could only be born from anger.

I saw the fire in her eyes, the defiance she had forced me to deal with since I first saw her.

"I'm not an animal. You say you want to marry me, yet keep me on an invisible leash."

My jaw tightened, and my cock stirred to life.

"What leash? I left you alone for not even an hour, and you tried to run away." Taking a few steps toward her, I saw her flinch.

Maybe I was getting through to her that I wasn't someone to mess with. Normally, I'd welcome that frightened look, but I hated that she feared me. I would never hurt her.

I strode toward her until her back was against the wall. Placing my hands on either side of Selena, I pulled her in close until our bodies nearly touched. Her breasts pressed against me, causing my cock to become rock-hard.

"You belong to me. You will do as I say, when I say, and how I say. You will accept all I give you, or I will take the payment in the form of your father's life." My words were harsh, and I took a step back, hoping she understood.

"I am a person. I have the right to live my life freely." She stepped away, but I followed and continued to glare at her.

"The only decision you get to make is how you want to please me."

"What?" Her eyebrows drew together.

"There are only two choices. I take decisions out of your hands and make them for you. You become my wife and let me take care of you. Protect you. Or..." I took a step back, "I make your cage smaller and smaller until you realize how good you have it."

She was working me up, and I didn't even recognize the things that came out of my mouth.

Her nostrils flared, and I knew my words meant nothing to her. She was like a wild animal and needed to be tamed.

"Take off your clothes, Selena, and sit on the edge of the bed."

Her emerald eyes widened as she hesitated but then said, "No."

"If you don't, then I take them off for you."

No more being patient with her. It was time she did what I said and learned she wasn't the one in charge.

Selena scoffed and crossed her arms. "You want me to take off my clothes? Fine." She pulled off her skirt.

Then, as if to taunt me, she slowly plucked at every button on her blouse. I stood there and waited as if it wasn't agonizing to watch her take her time.

Soon the silky blouse was on the floor, leaving only a white lace bra and thong covering her gorgeous body. I tried to look like I'd seen everything before, as if every woman's body was the same to me, but that wasn't true. It was a struggle just to keep my eyes on her face, but Selena was more beautiful than I ever imagined.

"Very good. Now, go to the edge of the bed." I pointed to the creamy silk-covered bed, the one I'd been waiting to share with her.

She did as I asked, and I watched her like a predator.

"Take off your underwear." I wasn't fucking around anymore.

Her hands shook as she hooked her thumbs under the thin straps and pushed them down to her ankles. I swallowed hard. My cock was like steel and so fucking ready to be inside her. I knew I should wait until our wedding night, but I didn't know if I could control myself around her anymore.

"Sit and spread your legs."

Her eyes rolled skyward as if she disagreed, but then did as I asked.

My cock throbbed as I stared at her pussy. Soft curls barely covered her. I could smell her heat and her want for me.

Goosebumps covered her soft, caramel-colored skin. Strands of hair covered her face, and it was the sexiest thing I'd ever seen.

I bit my tongue, trying to keep from ravishing every inch of her body.

Clearing my throat, I had to gain control.

I took off my tie and loosened my collar, then sat in the chair across from her.

Her eyes widened, and her hand flew to her chest. I knew it was the first time she'd seen the scar.

"You were shot?"

"That's right."

Her fingers traced the scar, and I ached to pull her into my arms and tell her everything about me. But not even my brothers knew me like that... not even Elba.

Selena didn't deserve my truths.

"Why?"

"It doesn't matter." I wanted to leave the past in the past.

"How did it happen?" Her voice was soft.

I ignored her words and let my fingers slide across her chest. Goosebumps broke out across the path I created, and when her nipples hardened, she pushed out her chest.

She wanted what I had to give. Licking her lips, Selena's eyes filled with lust.

"I have watched you for a long time, little dove. Longer than you realize."

She said nothing.

"I've seen how people have treated you. But I would never do to you what they have done. When I say I'll protect you, I mean it. My word is as solid as the marble that Michelangelo carved David from." I fell to my knees in front of her exquisite body. Leaning in, I kissed the slight rounding of her belly, and her legs trembled. Turning her head to the side, she placed a hand on my arm.

"I may not be the type of man you want, Selena." Her eyes searched my face, and I had to look away. "But you need me, even if you don't realize it yet. This is going to happen. We will be husband and wife."

That last part was more for me than for her. I had to control myself around her, but I needed more; I needed to taste her.

Dotting kisses down her belly to the small patch between her thighs, I pushed her legs farther apart. "Lean back." My voice darkened with need.

When she did, I groaned. Her pretty pink lips glistened in front of me. Selena was more beautiful than the most ornate flower—and she smelled even sweeter.

I sprinkled the faintest of kisses around her pussy, causing her to gasp. Her moan erupted when I slid my tongue across her swollen clit.

"Domenick." She sighed.

Her word was barely a whisper, but it broke something in me. Hearing my name on her lips turned me into the uncontrollable beast I had been holding back for so long.

I pressed a finger against her clit, causing her to whimper. Her pussy was so wet, I could feel her juices on my fingers. I moved my finger back and forth and watched as her hips moved with my hand.

The sexiest fucking thing I had ever seen was watching her please herself, but this was a close second with the sounds she made and the way her body responded to me. I leaned down, pressing my mouth against her pussy.

A fresh wave of her juices met my tongue. I flicked it over her clit, and the way she reacted had me harder than I'd ever been.

Pushing her legs open wider, I speared my tongue in and out of her sweet pussy. Her fingers curled through my hair, and she tried to push me back. I glanced up to see her eyes closed and lips swollen from biting them.

"You want me to stop?" I lifted my head and licked my lips, tasting her spicy honey.

Selena opened her eyes, and, with a dazed expression, she shook her head. "No. Please, don't stop."

That was all I needed to hear.

I slid two fingers inside her dripping core and sucked on her clit. Her hips rocked, and I had to place my arm over her to hold her in place. She was so small, I worried my cock might break her. I didn't want to hurt her, but I wanted to be inside her so badly.

Once she came, I had to leave. Because if I stayed, I'd end up fucking her, and I had to wait.

I added another finger, and her body tightened around me. It wouldn't be long before she came.

"Domenick," she moaned.

I gripped her hip with my hand and held her in place as I continued to kiss her pussy, lapping up her juices. "Don't make me stop. I want to feel you come for me. Can you do that for me, little dove?"

Selena nodded, and I knew she wouldn't last much longer.

She screamed my name, bucking against my hand, and I grabbed her waist with both hands, refusing to let her move.

When she finished, I stood. My breath was wild as my mind and cock argued for dominance.

Why should I wait to fuck Selena? Angel had always told me my future wife had to be pure, and I took his words to heart.

But standing over Selena, I realized there was no waiting. Today was the day I'd make her mine. I unzipped my pants and pulled them down, releasing my dripping cock.

Chapter 10

S elena

I had never felt pleasure like that in my life. My limbs were so weak, and when I tried to prop myself up on my elbows, my arms shook.

Domenick stood over me with his cock in his hand. "I need you to turn over, little dove. Lay on your belly."

I tilted my head. "But I don't understand—"

"It's not for you to understand. Remember, you do what you're told, and I take care of you." His jaw was tight as he bit out the words. "It's better this way for your first time."

My eyes widened. He knew I was a virgin.

"First time?"

I was embarrassed, though I shouldn't be. But at that moment, I wanted to be sexy for him, which was ridiculous because he kept me trapped like a pet. But the way he touched my body and made it come alive, I wanted to do that for him.

"Selena." He reached over and slid his finger across my jawline. "I told you I know you. You're beautiful just like this."

I was stunned. With Domenick, I felt treasured.

He straightened and gently helped me turn over. I glanced back and saw the Devil spread my thighs and lightly kiss the inside of my knee. He kissed his way up my thigh, stopping at my bottom, where he lingered, licking and teasing me. I squirmed.

He lifted his head. "Mine," he growled.

He moved up my body, kissing me softly. I was on fire. I wanted him so badly. But also, there was something else. Something deeper. It was as if I craved him, though I didn't understand why. I understood nothing about the whole situation. Why would someone like Domenick want me? He could have models and the most sophisticated women from anywhere in the world. Yet, he was here with me.

Maybe I shouldn't question it. I decided, since I was about to lose my virginity, I'd just be in the moment. Enjoy what this devastatingly handsome man could do to my body. I was ready for him to fill me.

"Please," I whispered.

Domenick grabbed my hips and lifted me until I was on my knees on the edge of the bed. Then he slapped my ass. That sweet burn rippled through me and caused my core to clench.

A moment later, his hand was sliding up my spine, and I shivered. "Don't tense up, Selena. Relax."

The intrusion hurt when his cock slid into my pussy. I cooed, but he pulled back and then pushed forward again. He felt my tightness and was determined to push through until I was dripping with pleasure.

He held on to my hips, guiding me with his hands until I was opening up to him. I was lost in the intense but lovely pleasure, giving me the best kind of pain.

His fingers dug into my skin. I glanced back to find him watching as his cock slid in and out of me. I inhaled the smell of his cologne mixed with our sex.

"You're so fucking tight." His face showed his extreme pleasure. He thrust hard and deep into me, and I cried out. "How does that feel, Selena?"

"Oh, God. It's so good." I closed my eyes. He pumped into me, setting a hard pace. He was rough, but the pressure made my nerves sizzle with desire.

He made me feel things I didn't know were possible. I squirmed against him, opening my legs wider for him.

Two of his fingers slid over my cheeks, down to my puckered hole, where he traced around. My skin tingled like it would split open.

What is he doing?

"You're going to like this, little dove."

Before I could respond, he pushed a finger into my asshole. I gasped at the slight burning, but once he moved his finger, the pain gave way to an intense pleasure.

I arched my back. "Yes."

"This is all new to you, so I'll take it easy on you."

I was so lost in bliss that I couldn't respond, and the sensation of being filled was intense.

He slowed down, taking his time. His cock slid in and out of my pussy, and the other finger pushed deeper into my ass. He transported me to another world. Domenick was gentle, but his dominance was like a force of nature.

I couldn't speak. My heart was pounding. I'd climaxed when he finger-fucked my ass, but that was just a prelude to the pleasure he was going to bring.

He pushed me forward, his finger still in my ass. I was on my forearms as he pumped his cock into me, bringing me to the edge of ecstasy. The feeling was so amazing, I thought my body was going explode I gripped the sheets in my fists. "Oh my God."

He slapped my ass, and I moaned. I wanted him to do it again.

He did, but this time, something built inside me so fast, all I could do was cry out his name: "Domenick."

I orgasmed again—something I didn't even realize was possible.

Domenick stilled. "Selena."

His head slumped forward, and he pumped into me a few more times before he gently pulled me into his arms. He crawled onto the bed so he was spooning me, then he pulled the covers over us. Once I was in his arms, my body relaxed.

Domenick was gentle as he kissed my neck. "You're so beautiful, little dove."

I didn't know what to say. It was all too much. I'd lost my virginity to a man I'd met less than a week ago. I didn't know what he was thinking or feeling. He was in complete control of me, and I was at his mercy.

This was not how I imagined it would be. I'd thought the guy would be awkward—a nervous virgin like me. I thought he'd worry about how I felt or if he was hurting me.

But Domenick had no such concerns. He knew what he wanted, and he knew how to get it. It was crazy.

I was a prisoner, but somehow... I never felt safer.

I was breathing hard, but the pleasure didn't subside. I could feel his heart pounding in his chest under my fingers.

"Selena?"

"Yes?"

"You're mine now. No one else's."

I knew what that meant, and for the first time since meeting him only four days ago, I liked it.

"I'm yours."

His hard cock was pressed against my ass, and while I couldn't see him, I imagined how he looked. The arrogance in his eyes. The confidence of a man who knew he was in control. A dangerous man who could take or give pleasure to me.

JOSIE MAX

Even though I feared him, I wanted him.

Chapter 11

D omenick

We fucked all night, but I left Selena sleeping in her hotel room.

Something was wrong with me. I couldn't think straight around her. She tasted so sweet, and I couldn't resist taking a bite.

As I stepped out into the hallway, I felt a strange pang in my chest. It wasn't the usual feeling of satisfaction after a good lay. It was something deeper, something more elusive. I tried to shake it off and headed toward my room, where I was meeting my brothers.

As I walked down the hallway, my thoughts kept drifting back to Selena. I knew I wanted to marry her for revenge, but now the idea of revenge was complicated. It would hurt Selena, and the last thing I wanted was her pain.

There was another reason for marrying her, which was to produce an heir. The way my brothers acted, I didn't think there would be a next generation. It was up to me to make sure the Satriano family continued.

When I got to my room, the door opened before me. There stood my guard Ricco, and beyond him, Elba and Vitale.

"Thought you'd stop by yesterday after arriving, but I guess you were having too much fun with your toy." Vitale chuckled as he swirled a tumbler of whiskey in his hand.

Who came to Italy only to drink whiskey?

I bit out, "Selena isn't a toy."

My brothers glanced at one another.

"Been there, Domenick. Be careful." Vitale shook his head. "Don't be fooled by their innocent act. You'd be surprised who'd sleep with you so they can go after your money."

I picked up my pace and headed straight for Vitale, but a hand stopped me.

Elba kept his hand on my chest as he moved in front of me. "Let it go. It's Vitale."

I stepped back, anger and frustration boiling inside my chest. I couldn't stand Vitale's constant disrespect toward women. It was as if he saw them as objects to be used and tossed aside. I knew Selena wasn't like that. She had a fire within her that blazed, and I couldn't wait until she was at my side wielding it.

"You need to learn some respect," I spat out. "Selena is not like the women you've been with. She's different, and I won't let you talk about her like that."

Vitale's expression softened, and he put his glass on the table. "I'm just looking out for you, Domenick. You know, the way you looked out for us with Dad."

He knew I never wanted to speak about our father, but Vitale was the one who knew everyone's buttons to push, even mine.

My nostrils flared. "Why are you here, Elba?"

He knew I didn't buy his bullshit about just wanting to visit Vitale.

"You know how I told you that Marko Dratshev showed up at The Golden Tower?"

"Yes."

"He stepped foot on our property again. Only this time, he had a woman with him."

Elba took his phone and held it out for me. There was a grainy picture of Marko with his arm around a woman. I tried to zoom in on the woman, but couldn't make her out.

"Who is this?"

Elba was silent longer than I liked.

"Elba, I asked you, who is this woman?"

"Angel's girlfriend, Eeva Feld."

My blood ran cold.

"We haven't seen her since—"

I cut Vitale off, "Since the day we found Angel stabbed to death."

Angel had a lot of enemies. Any rival gang could have put a hit out on him—my brothers suspected the Dratshev family. But what I found suspicious was that not only did Eeva disappear, but so did most of Angel's money.

I knew what this meant: Marko was sending a message. He was letting us know he had the woman who killed the only man I loved as a father.

Marko wanted my turf, which meant he wanted me gone for good. I knew him going to The Golden Tower was no accident.

I took a deep breath, trying to control the anger and fear that coursed through my veins.

"I think you were right, Domenick. Maybe Eeva did play a part in Angel's death," Elba said, and Vitale nodded.

It was time they saw what I knew to be true. Eeva's hands were dirty, and they'd never be clean as far as I was concerned.

"We need to take care of this. We can't let Marko get away with disrespecting us in this manner. He's crossed the line too many times."

Elba nodded. "I know. I've asked Iggy to keep an eye on him back in Chicago."

"We need to send a message... to show him we're not afraid," I said, my voice deepening with anger.

Elba nodded, knowing what I meant. We had to make an example out of someone. It was the only way to show Marko we were still in control. We were in Chicago first, and we ran the city. They arrived recently, and we'd let them stay.

But not anymore.

"Who do you have in mind?" Vitale asked, a smirk on his face.

I looked at Vitale, his smile making me want to punch him in the face. He always seemed to take pleasure in causing trouble, and I knew he was hoping for some bloodshed tonight.

I wanted to take Eeva out for what she did, but she was obviously too close to Marko, who ran the Dratshev family.

"Don't they have a cousin who went to DuPaul—"

Elba snapped his fingers. "Pavel."

I smirked. "Yeah, that little weasel. Doesn't he like to beat up his girlfriends?"

Vitale nodded. "Yes. He tried to go after my friend Jonny's sister a while back, but we put a stop to that. Now he stays over on his side of the line."

Vitale meant the south side.

I knew what we had to do. "Bring him to me."

Vitale's smirk turned into a wicked grin. I had a feeling he was enjoying the idea of causing chaos and mayhem, but I needed to send a message to Marko that he had gone too far this time.

"We're all heading back to Chicago, including you, Vitale. Your vacation in Italy ends now."

"Good. I was tiring of delicious food, excellent wine, and beautiful women, anyway."

95

I slapped my brother on the back of his head. "You need to take this more seriously. This is our family. We protect our own."

He rubbed the back of his head. "It was a joke. You need to lighten up."

I glared at my brother. His back-talk was pushing me to the edge. First Selena and now Vitale.

With my brother, he had always been a bit of a jokester. Vitale was someone who thought life was only to be enjoyed and rarely did what he was told. It wasn't just his fucking around with women that got him sent to Italy.

I hoped our connections in Florence would help set him straight, but that hadn't seemed to happen. "I'll lighten up when I'm dead. In the meantime, we focus on the problem with the Dratshevs that will soon be at our doorstep if we don't do something soon."

Elba nodded in agreement, his eyes dark with determination. "We'll have Pavel brought to you tonight. What do you want us to do with him?"

I thought for a moment. "Make it a public display. I want everyone in Chicago to know that the Satriano family is not to be messed with. And make sure Marko knows we're coming for him next."

Vitale grinned. "Now that's what I'm talking about."

I could see Elba wasn't as excited. "This won't go unnoticed, Domenick. We're starting a war."

"I know," I said solemnly. "But we can't let them come after us like this. We have to show them we're not weak."

My brothers nodded because they knew I was right. It was time to make a move, to show the Dratshevs we were still in control. And if that meant bloodshed, then so be it.

I appreciated that my brother was on top of things, but this was going to get ugly. I had to protect Selena from getting tangled up in our mess.

I turned to Elba and Vitale. "After the blood dries from Pavel, we turn our attention to Eeva. Then, find out what Marko is planning with her."

Elba nodded. "I'll reach out to my contacts."

Vitale finished his whiskey. "I'll watch Selena."

I clenched my jaw. I didn't like the idea of Vitale near her.

"No, I will."

As they left the room, I couldn't shake off the feeling in my chest. It was like a knot that wouldn't untangle. I knew I had to focus on the task at hand, but I couldn't stop thinking about Selena.

She was my weakness, my kryptonite. Every time I thought about her, my heart would ache. It was like she had a hold on me I couldn't shake off. I didn't want to bring her into this world of violence and bloodshed, but I had picked her for a reason—and not just to marry and keep the Satriano line going.

I had a deeper connection with her that even she didn't know about. And it seemed the connection was showing her face. The one thing I hadn't counted on was letting Selena get to me, but it seemed my heart had other plans with her.

I needed to clear my head, so I walked out to the loggia. The moon was full, casting a pale light over the rose bushes and statues. Glancing up to the balcony of Selena's room, I wondered if I should have acted so soon with her.

All the questions soon died when I saw movement in her room. There was more than one figure in her room, and an icy chill ran down my spine.

The silhouette wasn't my brother. The other person was short and about Selena's size. Not even Ms. Marta looked like that.

I quickly made my way toward the grand staircase, my heart racing with a mix of fear and anger. I knew something was wrong, and I couldn't let Selena get hurt.

I quietly drew the gun holstered at my waist and crept toward her door. I noticed it was ajar. When I pushed the door open, it hit the wall with a loud *thud*.

"Selena," I called out, but only silence answered.

I stepped into the room, gun at the ready. It was dark, the only light coming from the moon outside. I could hear faint footsteps in the distance, but I couldn't tell if they were coming toward me or moving away.

My heart was pounding in my chest, my grip tightening around the gun. I knew I had to be careful, but the thought of Selena being in danger made me reckless.

"Selena," I called out again, louder this time.

Still no answer.

After I searched every inch, I came to the horrible realization that Selena was gone.

Chapter 12

S elena

Something was very wrong.

The guy driving the car kept looking in the rearview mirror like he was nervous about something.

"And Mr. Satriano said he wanted me moved to his personal villa?"

If he had a villa in Florence, then why didn't he take me there from the airport?

Nothing about this added up.

"Yes."

The guy had a thick accent, but it wasn't Italian. It sounded different, like something I couldn't exactly place. I couldn't help but feel a sense of unease as the car weaved its way through the streets of Florence. The driver's constant glances in the rearview mirror only added to my growing suspicion that something wasn't quite right.

I had spent the past two days trying to get away from Domenick, and here I was, getting my wish. But I worried the solution might be worse than anything I had with Domenick.

The car came to an abrupt stop, and the driver turned to face me. His eyes were dark, and his expression was stern.

There was no villa anywhere in sight. We were definitely out of the city, but not in front of a building that looked lived in.

"You need to come with me," he said firmly.

Before I could protest, the driver hopped out of the car. He got to my door before I could get out and grabbed my arm, pulling me out of the car.

He was a large, intimidating figure with a thick build and broad shoulders. His face was expressionless, his dark eyes piercing and unreadable. I sucked in a breath, and his heavy, musky scent seemed to permeate his clothes, along with the faint whiff of alcohol.

We stood in front of a decrepit building that looked like someone had abandoned it years ago. I tried to pull away, but the driver's grip was too strong.

As we entered the building, I could hear faint whispers and footsteps echoing through the halls. The driver pushed me into a room filled with men in suits, all of whom were staring at me with cold, unfeeling eyes.

"Welcome," one man said, his voice laced with a heavy accent. "I trust your journey was comfortable?"

Fear and confusion had paralyzed me, and I couldn't comprehend what was going on.

The driver took me to a metal chair in the middle of the room and forced me to sit. I flinched when he yanked my hands behind the chair and tied me to it. I tried to pull away, but the rope was tight.

The man continued, "My name is Pavel. You're probably wondering why you're here."

I nodded, unable to speak.

Pavel walked over to me and brushed his hand against my cheek. His touch was repulsive, and I recoiled. "You're here because we need to have a little chat about your relationship with Domenick Satriano," he said, his voice cold and menacing.

If the driver was imposing, then Pavel was even more so. He had a thick beard, muscular build, and piercing eyes that caused me to shiver.

I swallowed hard, my throat dry. "What do you want from me?"

Pavel smiled, revealing a row of gleaming teeth. "We want you to spy on Domenick for us. His family is a little too greedy. We want a piece of the pie, but he doesn't like to share." His eyes drifted down my body.

I had been scared when I first met Domenick, but it was nothing like what I felt standing in front of Pavel. He was definitely younger than Domenick—I'd say he was closer to my age. Maybe it was his age, but I got the sense he wasn't as calm as Domenick. It looked as if he was itching to get his hands on me.

I knew I had to get out of there. But how? These men were dangerous, and I was in Italy and didn't speak the language.

"I won't do it," I said firmly, trying to sound brave.

Pavel chuckled. "Oh, my dear, you don't have a choice. Either you help us, or we'll make sure you never leave this place alive. A sign left for Mr. Satriano. That even he has a weakness."

My heart raced as I looked around the room, searching for an escape route, but there was none.

Suddenly, I heard a loud banging coming from outside. It sounded like someone had kicked the door in. The men in suits rushed toward the door, leaving me alone with Pavel.

"Don't even think about trying to escape," he said, baring his teeth like a wild dog.

I sat frozen, my eyes fixed on the door. Suddenly, a man burst into the room, tackling Pavel to the ground.

Domenick.

For a moment, everything slowed down, like I was witnessing it in slow motion.

Quick, rhythmic pops were followed by bullets ricocheting off the walls and floor until the entire room shuddered with an overwhelming cacophony of noise. Something hit me, and a pain bloomed from my chest and down my arm. The burning sensation was like a hot poker pressed against my skin. The heat radiated outward in waves, sending a sharp pain through my body.

I groaned and tried my best to keep my cries to myself as my arms urged to break free of their constraints. But Domenick must have heard because he glanced at me.

I shook my head, trying to communicate that I wasn't important right now. He was still fighting Pavel. But there was something in his eyes that darkened—a visceral anger that caused me to gasp. It changed something in Domenick. That was the only way I could describe it. A switch was flipped inside him.

The Devil made an appearance.

Domenick took a step back from Pavel, grabbed him by his hair, pressed his gun to his right eye and shot him dead.

The sound of Domenick's gun echoed through the room, followed by a deafening silence. I stared at him in shock, unable to believe what I had just witnessed. He turned to me, his eyes scanning my body for injuries, and rushed to my side.

The Devil disappeared, and Domenick took over, the man who had tasted me and took my virginity. The one who had given so much to me, no matter how much I fought him—he ran over to my side to give once again.

I was starting to question why I hated Domenick as he untied me. He showered me with clothes, jewelry, and anything I could want. Domenick treated me better than any guy I had known.

And the way he touched my body was something I didn't even know I wanted until he showed me.

He just risked his life for me, yet I had been trying to run from him since I first read his note to my father.

"You're hurt." His hands hovered over my wounds.

I nodded weakly, the pain making it difficult to speak. Domenick quickly ripped off a piece of his dress shirt and used it to stem the bleeding from my wounds.

"We have to get out of here," he said, urgency in his voice.

I tried to stand, but the pain was too much. Domenick scooped me up in his arms and carried me out of the building, his eyes scanning the surrounding area for any signs of trouble.

Once we were outside, a car door opened, and he placed me inside. No words were spoken until he came around next to me and the car took off.

"Anyone hurt?" Domenick asked the driver.

"Ricco."

Domenick cursed under his breath. "How bad?"

"He's dead."

My mouth fell open. Someone was killed because of me.

"No!" I cried out.

Domenick turned to me and brushed a lock of hair out of my eyes, then threaded his fingers through my hair. "You're safe."

I wiped the tears from my eyes. "He's dead because of me."

A bullet pierced the back of the car, causing me to flinch.

"Drive faster," he commanded.

The driver nodded and stepped on the gas, causing the car to swerve out of control. The wheels skidded and spun, leaving a trail of smoke in its wake as the car jerked and swerved down the street.

I clenched the door handle tightly with my good hand, but my bad shoulder slammed into the door, causing me to cry out in agony. I closed my eyes as the vehicle spun out of control, bouncing across the road as the sound of screeching tires filled the air. My head whipped back and forth, my stomach lurching with each bump, and my eyes stung with tears.

The car finally stopped, and I peeked outside to see that water surrounded us. I looked over at Domenick, who was staring out the window, his face full of shock and anger.

"They know about you," he said, still staring.

I stared back, unsure what to say to the man who saved my life. "What do you mean? They know about me? Who are *they*?"

I hadn't realized but the car hadn't come to a stop on the road. It fell into a lake.

The car was suddenly submerged in an icy, inky-black lake. The cold water slowly filled the cabin of the car as Domenick opened his mouth to say something, but no words escaped his lips. The car bobbed up and down as the lake's waves lapped against it. I could see nothing but darkness, except for a few glimmers of light from the streetlights above.

"We're sinking. We've got to get out."

I nodded. He tried to push open the door, but it wouldn't budge.

"The windows," he called out to the driver.

But there was no response. I leaned over and saw the driver was slumped over the steering wheel.

"I think he's dead," I said as shock caused my body to shake.

Domenick nodded, then reached into the driver's seat and pulled out the knife that had been wedged between the seat and the door. He positioned himself between me and the driver, opened the door, and removed the knife.

"Get behind me," he ordered.

"What are you going to do?" My body trembled at the thought of being out in the open water.

Domenick didn't answer. He held up the knife to the window between himself and the driver. He applied pressure to the glass until it finally gave way. Shards of glass cascaded down, breaking apart in the water and forming a cloud of sparkles. My body began to shake as I thought about what lay ahead, but Domenick remained stoic and determined.

Cold water rushed around us. The water was up to our chests, trying to push us down.

Domenick turned to me. "Grab my hand."

I nodded, but our heads were almost below water.

"Grab my hand, now!" Domenick yelled, tilting his head toward the last pocket of air.

I grabbed his hand. Stabbing pain from where I had been shot radiated through me as he yanked me through the window. When his grip loosened, I desperately tried to cling to his hand, but he pulled away.

Once I reached the surface, I gasped for air.

My body bobbed up and down as I called out for him, but only silence answered. All this time I tried to flee from him, but now I needed him more than ever. My heart thundered in my ears as warm tears slipped down my cheek, mixing with the icy water of the lake.

He was gone. The realization hit me so hard, I choked on the lake water. I tried to call him again, but the cold had robbed me of sound. The dark night had cooled off the heat of the day, making it feel like I broke into a freeze instead of the surface of a lake.

Then I felt something. Warm. Reassuring. Domenick was there, grabbing at my arm. I reached over and pulled him into a hug.

He was alive. Even now, in the middle of the cold lake, his other hand gently cupped my face. He was stronger than I could ever be.

"Can you swim?" His words were deep but gentle.

"Yes." I might have been a city girl, but my dad had an intense fear I would drown in Lake Michigan. So he took me to swim lessons at the local rec center every Saturday when I was a kid.

Even with my chest and shoulder hurting, I swam to the shore, and Domenick kept close beside me, reaching out every so often to let me know he was there. I lay on my back, feeling the warmth of the sand beneath me as it seeped into my clothes. I looked up at the sky, staring at the twinkling stars for what I thought would be the last time.

"You're okay. I've got you." Domenick lay next to me.

I turned to him, tears streaming down my face. "I thought I was going to die."

He leaned over and hugged me. "I won't let that happen."

The weight of everything came crashing down on me, causing me to sob into his chest.

"Shh." He held me tighter and petted my hair.

"I'm s-so scared." My teeth chattered as I buried my face in his chest.

"I'm here," he said, kissing the top of my head.

I felt like I was going to be sick. My vision blurred, and I felt myself slip away.

The last thing I remembered was the look of fear in Domenick's eyes.

Chapter 13

D omenick

"He's fucking dead." Vitale smiled as he leaned against the marble island in my kitchen, and all my brothers nodded in agreement.

My brothers killed all those men who tried to hurt Selena. Even Ricco had taken out two before they killed him.

The five of us stood around the kitchen island, dipping into antipasto platter Ms. Marta whipped up when we arrived a few hours ago. Trying to leave Florence had been a nightmare last night. The worst nightmare I could imagine. When I saw they had shot Selena, rage blinded me.

My blood boiled at the thought of Selena getting killed.

"And Selena?" Vitale's smile thinned.

"She's alive." My voice was hoarse from screaming at the medical staff I had to deal with in Italy last night.

"That was close," Elba said. "Ricco was killed, and they shot Selena. They know about her. Maybe that's why Marko is talking with Eeva."

My fingers, still trembling from the adrenaline of the night, slowly moved through my hair. It was matted with blood, and dirt was caked in, making it look almost auburn in the dim light of the rising morning sun.

"You should have left Selena back in that hospital in Italy," Iggy said.

I gritted my teeth. "The Dratshevs would have found her and finished the job. I had to fly her back with me."

She was never leaving my sight again. Never leaving my home.

When I carried her limp body into the hospital in Florence, the doctors and nurses raced around her, doing everything in their power to help her. Waiting for her to get out of surgery felt like an eternity. They managed to remove the bullet and told me she needed time to heal.

She would live. But for how long?

If I left her in that hospital room, another Dratshev goon would get to her. I couldn't risk it. The doctors protested when I took her, but even they couldn't stop me.

I was an idiot to think she meant nothing to me. As head of the Satriano family, I kept my feelings for anyone at a distance, but then came Selena... She changed everything.

She may not be my blood, but she was my heart. I'd protect her at all costs.

Vitale nodded. "We'll increase the security around the place. Nobody gets in without my say-so."

"Agreed," I said. "But we need to find out who betrayed us. Who told the Dratshevs about Selena? Or that we were in Italy with her."

"I, uh... I think I can find that out," Elba said with unease in his voice.

He was hiding something, but I didn't have the patience to figure out my brother's secrets right now.

I clenched my fists. "Don't think, just do. And once you discover who it is, they will pay for what they've done."

"That's right, D," Iggy said. "Nobody fucks with the Satriano family."

I looked around at my brothers, their faces grim with determination. I knew I wasn't alone; we were all in this together. They were ready to do whatever it took to protect our family.

I turned to Vitale. "Make sure Selena has everything she needs. And nobody, I mean *nobody*, gets close to her without my permission."

Vitale nodded, the smile on his face replaced with a look of seriousness. "Consider it done, D. I'll make sure she's safe."

"All of you are staying here in the big house until this gets sorted."

They all nodded, except for Elba.

I strolled over to him and folded my arms. "You got somewhere you need to be?"

"No. Of course not." He cleared his throat. "I'm staying here with everyone."

I kept my eye on him for a few moments before nodding.

It was going to be a long road ahead, but I was ready for it. Ready to protect Selena and my family at all costs.

As I walked out of the kitchen, I couldn't shake off the feeling of unease that had settled in my stomach. Something wasn't right, and I couldn't tell what it was. Whoever had betrayed us was still out there, lurking in the shadows.

I needed to find them before they could do any more damage.

But first, I needed to check on Selena.

As I climbed up the stairs to her bedroom, my mind raced with a million different thoughts. The image of Selena lying on the hospital bed, pale and lifeless, flashed before my eyes.

With a heavy heart, I made my way to the room where Selena was resting. The sight of her frail form on the bed sent a jolt of pain through me.

Her eyes fluttered open as I approached, and a small smile graced her lips. "Hey," she said weakly. Her skin was ashen and colorless, with a ghostly pallor that made her look like a porcelain doll. She had lost so much blood last night.

But it was her voice, which I hadn't heard since we left that small body of water outside Florence last night, that caused relief to flood through me. "Hey yourself," I replied, taking her hand in mine.

"I'm sorry," she whispered. "I never wanted to bring danger to your family."

I shook my head, brushing a strand of hair away from her face. "It's not your fault. We'll deal with whoever did this, but for now, you need to rest and recover."

Selena nodded, her eyes closing once more. "Thank you, D omenick... for everything."

My eyes closed in guilt. My selfishness and hate had brought her here—hell, it almost got her killed.

"No, don't thank me."

She smiled and reached her hand up to my lips. "Stop. You act so tough. And, yeah, you are brutal when you need to be. But you're also good when you need to be. You saved my life."

I stared at her, the warmth of her hand on my lips sending shivers down my spine. "I'll always protect you," I whispered.

She opened her eyes and looked at me with a mixture of vulnerability and hope. "Always?"

"Always," I repeated, leaning in to press my lips to hers.

The kiss was gentle at first, but as I deepened it, I felt her body respond. She was still weak, but there was no denying the attraction between us.

After we broke the kiss, I couldn't help but feel a sense of guilt. Her life was in danger, and here I was, getting lost in the moment. But then I saw the way her eyes sparkled with emotion, and I knew I couldn't resist her.

I pulled her into my embrace, my arms wrapping around her torso as I held her to my body. She was safe now, and that was all that mattered.

But the guilt was still there, a nagging feeling at the back of my mind. I needed to find out who was informing Marko about Selena.

I needed to make them pay.

As I held Selena in my arms, I made a vow to myself. I would do whatever needed to keep her safe, even if it meant sacrificing everything.

I was the head of the Satriano family, and I would not rest until I spilled their blood. But for now, I would focus on Selena. She needed me, and I needed her.

Together, we would face whatever came our way.

I watched her drift back to sleep. My eyes burned from lack of sleep, and my body begged me to rest. But there was someone I needed to meet with first before I'd get any sleep.

It was time to visit Selena's father.

Chapter 14

S elena

It had been a week since we got back from Italy. Domenick told me they had shot me near the shoulder, and if the bullet had been just an inch to the left, I could have died.

I didn't remember the flight home or much of the next few days. But I did remember waking up a few days ago with my father smiling down at me. Domenick had gone to get my dad and bring him to live in the house with us.

I felt so much relief having him here. We weren't allowed to leave the property, but being with my dad was, in some ways, like it used to be.

I'd cook us a big meal, and we'd eat and discuss the day. It was a little different having Ms. Marta there helping in the kitchen, and Domenick and his brothers joining us, but different in a good way.

I adored being part of this extensive family—it felt comforting. And I could tell Dad enjoyed swapping jokes with Vitale.

It was two weeks ago today when I walked in on Domenick in my kitchen, yet it felt like years had passed. I was afraid he was going to harm me, but he kept his promise—he would let no one hurt me. He earned my father's respect when I told him what happened in Italy.

My fingers brushed over the leaves of a bush in the back garden. Domenick's home was immense, and the backyard was quite large for being just outside Chicago. I guess he could afford an enormous property.

There was a whistle coming from the brick wall toward the end of the back garden. My eyes flickered up toward the tall trees lining the wall, looking for the bird that let out the call. I shook my head and took in a healthy breath of fresh air.

Domenick told me we were to be married soon, and it didn't scare me anymore. It actually excited me to become his wife.

I glanced back to see Elba standing on the terrace overlooking the backyard. There were always eyes on me, even in the house.

I lifted the apple Ms. Marta had given me right before I headed out into the backyard. Then I heard the whistling again, but this time, it didn't sound like a birdsong. Before I could take a bite, I moved closer to the tree line. I gasped at a shadow moving behind a tree.

When I looked back, I noticed Elba on his phone. My heart pounded in my chest when I realized something was off about the whole situation. Elba had always been so vigilant in keeping an eye on me, but he seemed distracted now. Was someone else watching me instead?

"Selena," a voice whispered from the trees.

"Who's there?" I took a step back and dropped the apple, ready to run.

I would not be tricked by some Russian guy again. This was Domenick's property, and there were so many people with guns that anyone from the Dratshev family would be stupid to come here.

Before I could turn and run, a woman stepped out from behind a tree. Everything in me stilled, especially my heart.

"Mom?"

The wrinkles around her eyes had deepened since I last saw her, and tears filled her eyes. I didn't remember her wearing so much makeup, but my memories of her were clouded.

I had so many questions for her. Why did she leave us? Why didn't she love me? But I settled on, "Why are you here?"

"To help you, baby." She opened her arms, expecting me to come running into her embrace. Yeah, that wasn't happening.

I didn't move. I couldn't. It had been years since I last saw her, and now she was just standing there, acting like nothing had happened. She broke my heart when she left us without a word, and I didn't know if I could forgive her.

"Why now?" I asked, my voice low and strained. "After all these years, why did you come back?"

"I tried to come back before, but your father, uh... never mind." She pursed her red-stained lips.

That made little sense.

"Dad would have told me if you tried to come back."

She sighed. "There's a lot of things your father keeps from you, Selena. I heard what happened to you in Florence."

What's going on?

I folded my arms over my chest. "Dad tells me everything."

"Did he tell you about making the deal with the Devil?"

I nibbled on my lower lip. He hadn't told me about that until I found the note in our mailbox.

Then there was the information about Mom stealing his money. He kept that from me too. But that was to protect me. Right?

"He only did that to protect me."

Her brows went up. "And here you are, captive in a mafia boss's home, recovering from being shot. How is that being protective?"

I rubbed my brow. I hated that she made sense.

"I'm not a captive. Domenick is protecting me."

Mom snorted. "Protecting you? He's a *criminal,* Selena. He's using you for his own gain."

"He's not using me. He wants to marry me." I glared at her. "And you don't know him like I do."

"I know enough." She took a step toward me, but I stepped back.

"I don't want to hear it. Domenick has a plan." I clenched my fists.

"A plan?" She raised an eyebrow. "Do you honestly think he's going to be able to take on the Dratshev family? They're too powerful."

How did she know anything about the Dratshev family? Domenick informed me a few days ago that it was the Dratshevs who kidnapped and shot me. They wanted to hurt me.

My head was spinning. "I-I don't know what to believe anymore."

"You need to come with me, Selena. You'll be safer with me." She reached out to touch me, but I flinched away.

"I'm safe here," I hissed.

She shook her head. "You don't understand. They're going to kill you. Domenick is going to use you as leverage, and when he's done with you, he'll discard you like trash."

"You don't know that." I backed away from her.

"I do know that, Selena. Did you know he killed his father because he got in the way? He was done with him too, and then Domenick murdered him with his own hands."

I gasped. That couldn't be true. I had heard so many things about Domenick, but I knew they were rumors to make him sound evil. Not like the man I knew.

Then that conversation we had when I tried to pull a knife on him popped up in my head. He mentioned having no problem taking out family if he needed to.

Was my mom telling the truth?

"You're lying," I said, my voice shaking. "He would never do that."

"Am I?" She tilted her head, her expression unreadable. "Think about it, Selena. You're just a pawn in his game. He doesn't care about you; he only cares about power."

I backed away from her, feeling like the ground was slipping beneath my feet. What if she was right? What if I was just a pawn in his game, a means to an end?

He even said he never made deals, but then he made a deal with my dad for me.

He lied.

"Selena, please." She reached out to me again, but I stepped back. "Let me take you away from here. I know someone who can help you. He helped me."

I shook my head. "I can't leave. I can't just abandon Domenick and Dad."

"Of course your father would side with Domenick. He owes Domenick so much money. I regret not taking you with me when I left; I should have never left you in your father's care. That was my fault, and I'll regret that for the rest of my life. But I'm here now. Selena, listen to me—" she started, but then a gunshot rang out.

My heart jumped into my throat as I spun around, trying to locate the source of the sound. Elba was gone from the balcony, but a few men were running out the back of the house toward me.

"We've got to go, now." She reached for my hand, but this time, I didn't jump back.

What if everything she had told me was true? That both my father and Domenick had been lying to me. That the man who wanted to marry me was just using me.

He was the type of man who would do something like that. This whole Dratshev and Satriano feud started because Domenick wanted full control of the city. He craved that power.

This time, I took her hand.

I felt a wave of fear wash over me as we ran into the forest. My mind was racing with thoughts of betrayal and deception. But I couldn't shake off the feeling that maybe, just maybe, my mother was right.

We ran for what felt like hours, the sound of footsteps chasing us all the while. My legs burned with the effort, but I didn't dare stop. I had to keep moving.

Finally, we came to a stop at a small clearing surrounded by trees. My mother glanced around, scanning the area for anyone who might hurt us. "I think we lost them," she said, her voice barely a whisper.

I leaned against a tree, my breaths coming in ragged gasps. I looked up at my mother, trying to make sense of everything that had just happened.

"Why did you leave?" My eyes seared her. "Why did you abandon us?"

Her back was to me, and she didn't move. "I told you... It was because of your father."

"No, you really didn't tell me. You just said Dad didn't tell me everything."

Her shoulder sank, and she turned. All the fear and sadness that etched her features earlier were gone. I could hardly believe it, but she appeared annoyed with my questions.

Before I could ask anything else, I heard footsteps. I pushed against the tree and stood straight, ready to run again.

"Mom, someone's coming," I whispered and reached for her hand.

"I know..." Her voice was low.

She never took my hand; instead, she stepped away and called out, "Marko?"

"Eeva. I'm here," a man with a thick Russian accent said from behind me.

My eyes widened as he moved around and took my mom into his arms, leaning in to kiss her.

Marko? Was this Marko Dratshev, the head of the Dratshev family? The same guy who sent his goons to try to kill me?

I took a step back, my heart pounding in my chest. What was going on? Why was my mother with the man who tried to kill me?

"Selena," my mother said, turning to me, "this is Marko Dratshev. He's the one who saved my life."

Saved her life? I shook my head in disbelief. This was too much to handle.

"How can you be with him? He's the one who tried to kill me."

"I didn't try to kill you, Selena. I tried to get you away from Domenick, but my cousin fucked it up."

My mother's eyes flickered back toward where we came. "I hate to do this, Selena, but we have to go."

"I don't want to go with him. Mom?" Was she really going to make me go with another criminal? She went on about how dangerous Domenick was, but then she brought me straight to Marko.

He turned to my mother and lowered his voice. "I thought she was going to be drugged..."

My eyes widened, but I pretended not to hear him.

"That's what Marta told us. That she would give her food to make her drowsy. I guess she lied."

Were they talking about Ms. Marta? I glanced at my hands. *The apple.* I wondered why she was so insistent I have a snack while out in the garden.

Marko nodded at my mother, and she reached into her jacket pocket and pulled out a syringe.

"What the hell are you doing..." My words died in my mouth as she stabbed me in the arm with the needle. Within seconds, my world turned black.

Chapter 15

Domenick

I rubbed my face with the towel after stepping out of the shower. Staring in the mirror, I felt a sense of relief, as if the weight of years of burden was melting away.

What was making me feel that way?

Selena.

What happened in Italy scared me. I felt as if my world would end if I lost her.

That was when it hit me that I loved her. Over the past few days, I tried to explain that feeling as protection of what was mine. But I had never been on edge like that for anyone.

I took a deep breath and closed my eyes, trying to focus on my emotions. The realization that I loved Selena was an overwhelming wave of emotions I had never felt before. I opened my eyes and stared at my reflection in the mirror. The man staring back at me was no longer the same person. The universe had shifted, and everything had changed... all because of Selena.

I knew I wanted to marry her. I knew I loved her. But did she feel the same?

Sucking in a breath, I knew I had to tell her. No matter how she felt, I wanted her to understand that I meant what I said when I told her I would protect her. That I would do anything to keep the woman I loved safe.

I ran my hand through my damp hair and turned to grab my clothes from the hanger on the door. I slid on the crisp white shirt, and as I buttoned it up, I imagined Selena helping. I smiled at the thought of her delicate fingers sliding over my sharp collar.

Once I put on my dark navy-blue jacket and trousers, I slipped on my Italian leather loafers, ready to make my way over to Selena's room. My mind raced with all the likely scenarios of how Selena would react. Would she reciprocate my feelings, or would I just end up scaring her away?

Opening the door to leave my room, I crossed the hall but hesitated as I reached for her bedroom doorknob. After taking a deep breath, I twisted the knob and slowly pushed the door open. The room was brightly lit, with only the sunlight seeping in through the sheer curtains.

"Selena," I called out.

There was no response. Stepping farther inside, I searched the bathroom. She wasn't in there.

I went back to her bed and opened the drawer to her bedside table. There was a small black notebook.

What I read inside stunned me.

She wrote about how she hated me, about her plans of getting away and trying to leave. There was an entry about my brother Elba telling her he'd help her escape.

The final entry was today.

Today is the day I find the courage to leave. I can't live with Domenick. He's a monster, a killer. I'll run until he can't find me.

What. The. Fuck.

I slammed the notebook on the table and made my way toward the balcony that overlooked the backyard—where Elba was on duty.

My blood boiled as I made my way out of the room. I trusted Elba, yet he betrayed me. The thought of Selena leaving me made me feel sick. I had to confront him.

As I approached the balcony, I saw Elba standing there, his eyes fixed on something in the distance. He turned as he heard me approach.

"Were you—"

"She took her," he cut me off, his breath coming out in ragged puffs.

My heart dropped as his words hit me like a ton of bricks. "Who took her? What are you talking about?" I demanded, feeling as if someone had ripped the ground out from underneath me.

Elba's face paled as his eyes widened with fear. "Eeva. I saw her."

My brows shot up. "And you did nothing to stop her?"

"I tried to shoot, but then realized I might hit Selena, so I stopped. I sent the guards on the ground after her."

Then a thought hit me. Was she kidnapped... or did Selena want to leave?

"Why did you tell Selena you'd help her escape?"

My brother's eyes widened. "I didn't tell her that... Oh wait, back in Italy. When I first ran into her." He shook his head. "I didn't know why she was there, so I thought she was a spy for the Dratshevs. I was going to take her and interrogate her. Then I realized she was Eeva's daughter and why she was here."

Was that why Selena wanted to escape? She must have found out why I wanted to keep her. And why I wanted to marry her.

I gritted my teeth, my fists clenched at my side as I tried to process everything Elba had just told me. My mind was racing, trying to piece together the reasons Selena would want to leave me.

I turned to face Elba, my eyes blazing with anger. "Why the fuck didn't you tell me this earlier?"

"Once she was kidnapped, it slipped my mind," Elba replied, his voice low and filled with regret. "After what happened to her, I could tell she had changed her mind."

What he didn't know was she hadn't changed her mind. And based on what just occurred in the backyard, I was right. She was planning an escape.

Was Selena just trying to protect herself, or was she trying to protect her mother? Maybe I was wrong about her. She wasn't an innocent daughter Eeva hurt by abandoning her. Eeva and the Dratshevs must have known I was coming for Selena, and now, they got her.

I rubbed my brow as I realized she said yes to me, taking her role as her father's payment a little too easily.

I turned to Elba. "We need to find her. Now."

He nodded, his eyes filled with determination. "I'll gather the men, and we'll start searching the area."

"Tell Rohon, Selena's father. Either he helped and knows something, or he doesn't and can help find her."

My brother nodded. I clenched my jaw as I watched him leave, my mind racing with all the possibilities of what could have happened to Selena. My heart pounded in my chest as I made my way down the stairs and out the door.

The sun was high in the sky, causing beads of sweat to line my brow. I took a deep breath, trying to calm my racing thoughts, but it was useless. The only thing that mattered now was finding Selena.

I heard my men call out her name, their footsteps echoing in the empty yard. I joined them, calling out her name, my heart thundered with fear and anger.

130

As we searched, my mind kept going back to the notebook I found in her room. The thought that she had been planning to leave me all along made me feel sick to my stomach. I just couldn't help but wonder if there was more to it than that.

The back gate was open, so that was where I went. There was a dirt path that led to a forested area. When I bought this place, the seclusion despite being so close to Chicago captivated me.

But now I realized anyone could easily slip in or out of my place without being noticed. Ripping off my jacket, I rolled up my sleeves and took off running.

The sound of twigs snapping under my feet filled the air as I ran deeper into the woods. My heart pounded in my chest as I tried to keep my thoughts under control. I couldn't let the fear and anger consume me. Not now, not when I needed to focus on finding Selena.

I ran for what felt like hours until I reached a small clearing in the woods. It was empty, but I could see footprints in the soft soil. They were fresh, and I knew they had to be Selena's.

I followed the footprints, my mind tumbling with fear and anger. What had happened to her? Was she hurt? Had she been taken by the Dratshevs?

As I ran, the sounds of my men calling out her name echoed in the distance. They were getting closer, but I could tell I was ahead of them. I had to find her before they did.

I pushed myself harder, my breaths coming out in ragged gasps. Then I came to a stop as something metallic glittered on the ground near a tree. As I tried to get my breath under control, I leaned down to pick up the object.

It was the necklace with the golden heart. The one Selena was holding when I confronted her in her closet. She looked as if she had never seen anything so beautiful, and I had thought the same thing about her.

I swallowed.

I pointed out the footprints as some of my men showed up. They ran off, leaving me alone to contemplate my next move.

I knew what I was going to do.

Since she was working with Eeva to destroy the Satriano family, then I'd punish her for it. It wouldn't be the punishment she'd be used to. This time, it wouldn't be my hand spanking her...

This time, I'd use my gun.

Chapter 16

S elena

The door to the black Land Rover opened, and a hand reached inside, grabbing my arm and yanking me out. I had woken up just moments ago and felt unstable on my feet.

"Where am I?" I mumbled.

My head was in a fog as I glanced around. The sun was setting, but I could make out the beige brick building I stood in front of. I was back in Chicago, but this wasn't my neighborhood.

I recognized nothing as I glanced around. Maybe this wasn't Chicago but another city. Ugh. I shook my head, trying to focus.

"Inside," a man shouted.

Recognizing the voice, I reared my head back. It was Marko. He was the one who pulled me out of the car. His grip on my arm tightened until I flinched.

A smile appeared on his face as he tugged me along. "I'm not like Domenick; I don't spoil women."

I stumbled and tried to keep up as we moved inside the building. It was an apartment building, and we passed the row of metal mailboxes that lined the wall.

The place looked like it hadn't been updated since the last century. The brown vinyl flooring was cracked, with pieces missing here and there. The walls were a deep yellow, with peeling paint and grime. The mildewy odor of stagnant air and cigarette smoke filled the corridor.

"Selena," my mom's voice came up beside me.

That was right. It was all coming back to me. My mom came to rescue me. She told me Marko would help.

"Mom. What's going on?"

"Sweetie," she pushed some hair out of my face, "you're going to live here. And you're here to help me."

I shook my head, about to ask more questions, but a door opened, and I was thrown inside. Stumbling forward, I couldn't get my footing and fell onto the rough burgundy carpet. I frowned. It smelled even worse in here, like piss and beer.

"Mom?" I looked around and saw an old, worn couch and a small wooden table. The curtains were closed, so the only light came from the open front door. When I glanced back at the front door, I saw Marko and my mom standing there.

"There will be food soon, I promise." My mom didn't even smile when she spoke. She seemed so sweet and apologetic back in Domenick's backyard, but now she was different. Colder.

A sense of dread washed over me as they closed the door behind them. What the hell was going on? Why was I here? My mom left me so long ago without a word, and then she came back to save me out of the blue?

I had too many questions to count.

I got up from the floor and walked over to the window. After pushing back the curtains, I tried to open the sliding glass door, but it was stuck shut. The room was dimly lit, and the stench was almost unbearable. I took a deep breath and tried to ignore it.

As I looked outside, I saw a group of men standing around in the parking lot, smoking and laughing. They seemed to be watching the building, waiting for something. I wondered if they were part of my mother's plan.

Suddenly, I heard footsteps outside the door. My heart started racing as the door opened and Marko walked in.

He was holding a paper plate of food in his hand. "Here," he said, handing it to me.

I looked down and saw a sad excuse for a meal. It was some burned toast with an opened can of tuna.

He stood there and stared at me once I took the plate. "The only reason you're alive right now is because of Eeva. I wanted to kill you, but she told me you would help us."

135

Maybe my mother was trying to help me...

I went over to the table and set down the plate. "I don't understand why you would want to kill me?"

"You're the Devil's wife." Marko waved his hand at me. "He needs to know the Dratshevs mean business. If we want in on the west side of Chicago, we will take it. We will keep removing the ones he loves until he complies. He loved Angel, and now Angel is dead. He loves you..."

Marko didn't finish. He left me there to figure out his words, but I wasn't an idiot. I may not have known who Angel was, but I could guess she was his love. She was the one who had captured his heart.

I was just a sad replacement. Someone he could fuck and pretend it was Angel. And here I was, falling for Domenick. I wanted to tell him I loved him, that I wanted to marry him.

But I was foolish to believe I could ever capture his heart.

I wrapped my arms around myself. "He doesn't love me."

"I don't care. All I care about is getting him to back off the west side neighborhood. He wants something from you, and if I torture you enough, I can get that out of you. Find out what exactly he likes about you."

Torture? Hot tears streamed down my cheek as I watched Marko turn and open the front door to leave. My mother stood just outside, and I cried out for her, but she threw her head back and laughed while wrapping her arm around Marko.

The door closed, and I stood there in the disgusting room, realizing my mom had tricked me.

She never loved me. I had denied it all my life, but there was no denying it now. The woman hated me.

Even when I was a kid and she was still around, she'd ignore me whenever Dad left for work. I remembered crying for her attention. Begging her to take me to the library or the park, but she'd be too busy on the phone, talking to a friend. Or she'd tell me to shut up so she could watch one of her shows.

When she left, my heart broke, but it wasn't as much of a surprise to me as it was to Dad.

I sat there, feeling lost and alone. The thought of being tortured scared me, but even more, the thought of being used as a pawn to hurt Domenick made me sick to my stomach. I had to get out of here. I had to warn him and stop my mother and Marko.

I got up from the table and started pacing, my mind racing. I needed a plan, but my thoughts were jumbled and disorganized.

Suddenly, the door burst open, and two men walked in. They were rough-looking, with tattoos covering their arms and scars on their faces. I could smell the alcohol on their breath as they approached me.

"What's a pretty little thing like you doing in a place like this?" one of them sneered.

My heart raced as I backed away, but they grabbed me and pushed me against the wall. Their hot breath landed on my neck as they pawed at me.

"Get off me!" I screamed.

But they just laughed and held me tighter.

Just when I thought things couldn't get any worse, the door opened again. This time, it was my mother.

"Let her go."

The men slowly backed off me, and I slid down the wall, sobbing.

"I never wanted you, Selena. I never wanted your father. Getting knocked up at nineteen was not in the plans for me."

Anger boiled up inside as I listened to her words. How could someone be so heartless? "You're pathetic. Boo-fucking-hoo," I spat at her.

She sneered and slapped me across the face. I rubbed my cheek. *Fuck her.*

For so long, I wondered if I had done something to make her run off. Was I not good enough or sweet enough?

Now, I realized it was her all along.

"You ungrateful bitch. I didn't want you, but I fed you and put a roof over your head. When it was winter, I made sure you had a warm coat."

I gave her a slow clap as I stood. "Congratulations. You did the bare minimum. You know who else makes sure people are fed, clothed, and have a roof over their heads?"

Her brow rose. "Churches?"

I shook my head. "Prisons." I chuckled. "Even Marko brought me some toast."

"You're lucky I don't kill you myself," my mother snarled, her eyes blazing with fury.

I looked at her with disgust. "You brought me here to torture me? To use me as a pawn to hurt Domenick?"

She shrugged. "He's not the first and won't be the last man to fall for a pretty face. Domenick is a ruthless man who killed his father."

My brows shot up.

"Oh, what? You thought I made that up, Selena? I may have fed you some lies to follow me into the woods, but that one was the truth. He killed his own flesh and blood."

There must have been a reason. Domenick wouldn't do that unless he had to.

"I didn't kill your father, but there were many times I wanted to." She rolled her eyes. "But I'm not sick like Domenick; I don't kill someone just because. And what about your landlord? I heard about that one."

He murdered him. While I wasn't sad about my landlord getting what he deserved, I didn't understand why Domenick would be so brutal about it.

"He did it to protect me." I hated how she thought she was better than Domenick, because she wasn't. No, she was so much worse.

She looked around. "What about now? Where is he now? Oh, that's right. He's not protecting you. I easily got into his backyard."

I blinked, wondering how that was possible.

"Even his own family let us know about you. Domenick doesn't want to protect you, Selena. Men like Domenick can't love women like us—they're incapable of those feelings. If you don't believe me, just look at what he did to his dad."

"What do you mean, women like us? I'm nothing like you. I didn't abandon Dad."

She stepped close and placed her hand on my cheek, right where she had slapped me. "Oh, sweetie. You do not know what kind of woman you are." She leaned in closer, her breath hot against my ear. "You're just like me. You're willing to do whatever it takes to survive, to get what you want."

I pulled away from her, disgusted. "I will never be like you."

She just laughed. "We'll see about that. But for now, I need you to do something for me. I need you to call Domenick and tell him you're leaving him. Tell him it's over between you two."

I stared at her in disbelief. "Why would I do that?"

"Because if you don't, I'll kill him." She said it so casually, like it was nothing.

My heart sank at her words. "You can't do that."

"Oh, I can, and I will. I killed his precious Angel, and he was more protected than Domenick. But you don't have to let him die, as long as you do what I say."

Chapter 17

D omenick

Three days had passed with no clues about Selena's whereabouts. Yesterday, she called and left a message, telling me how she left and wasn't coming back.

But I heard the fear in her voice, and I knew something was off. I knew what she said in the message was true, but I couldn't shake the feeling that there was something more to it. We followed up on every lead, but all we found were dead-ends or locations where she hadn't been.

I lifted the whiskey to my lips and took a sip. Sunlight twinkled off the crystal glass, causing the amber liquid to glow.

I had barely slept since she'd been gone. The thought that she used me ate me up inside.

And yet, I just wanted to hold her again.

"It's nine in the morning," Elba said as he leaned against my office door.

I didn't look up, just watched the whiskey swirl in my glass. "Any news?"

My brother sighed as he strolled into the room. "You need to rest. And for god's sake, drink something that doesn't have the word *proof* in the description."

My lips thinned as I tossed back the whiskey. The harsh burn down my throat felt like the punishment I deserved.

"I put our family at risk by bringing her here."

I put my heart at risk too.

My brother looked toward the window. He knew I was right and didn't have the heart to tell me.

"Maybe," he finally spoke. "But the heart can guide you only so far. Eventually, you have to use your eyes too."

I smirked and leaned back in the leather chair. "When did you get so smart?"

"Since I witnessed the evil game of love play out in front of my eyes."

He must have meant when I killed our father. My brother didn't take the wrath from our father as much as I did, so he questioned my solution for years. Believing I took it too far.

But he hadn't witnessed what I had. Where Elba hid in the background from my father, my youngest brother didn't.

I knew what I had to do so Luca would live.

Neither Luca nor I spoke about the reasons I killed our father. Therefore, Elba came to his own conclusions, and he'd resented me for what I did ever since.

"I love my brothers, and I will do anything to protect them."

He nodded but wouldn't look at me. "I do too. And for that reason, I am focused on finding Selena."

Maybe I should forget about her. I had done so much damage because of my obsession with hurting Eeva for what she did to Angel.

"She betrayed me, Elba." I shook my head. "She was a means to an end. I know Eeva killed Angel, and I thought if I kidnapped and married her daughter, then her greed would cause her to come to me. Then I'd do to her what she did to Angel."

"That was your plan?"

I nodded. "Not just that. I knew we needed to grow our family. I have four brothers, yet none of you look like you'll be settling down soon or ever, especially not Vitale."

Elba chuckled. "You're probably right, Domenick."

"I know I'm right. It's not as if Selena means anything to me," I lied to my brother.

He was silent once again. We sat there and let the hard reality of the past few weeks swirl in our heads.

"Stop keeping the truth from me," he said, shaking me from my thoughts of Selena.

"I don't lie to you, Elba."

"You just did. You said Selena meant nothing to you, yet you were willing to die for her back in Florence. Running straight into that building where you knew she was being held to save her."

"I promised to keep her safe, and I always keep my promises."

Elba's jaw ticked. "You promised to protect your family, yet you killed Dad. He was your family too."

I didn't flinch at his words. I had heard it all before, but I knew I had to make Elba understand the truth.

"I did it to protect Luca. Our father was going to kill him, and I couldn't let that happen. You wouldn't understand because you weren't there."

Elba's eyes narrowed. "You don't get it, Domenick. I *was* there, but I didn't see it the way you did. You always thought you were the only one capable of protecting us, but you were wrong. I could have helped too, if you had just given me a chance. I'm only a year younger than you."

I felt the weight of his words hit my chest. He was right. Maybe I had made things worse by taking on everything myself. But I couldn't dwell on the past; I had to focus on the future and find Selena.

"I'm sorry," I said, realizing my brother was right. "I was young, and I thought I had to protect all of you."

"You still think like that. And yet, here I am, ready to help."

I nodded, the weight of a thousand pounds lifting from my shoulders at my brother's words.

"And as for Selena... I've seen the way she looks at you. The woman loves you. If she's using you, then she's a damn talented actress, because she even fooled me."

I sighed. He didn't understand. My brother had never fallen for a woman who broke his heart. Elba was too cautious to let that happen.

"Then she fooled both of us."

"Did she?"

My nostrils flared, and I stood. "Yes. I found a black notebook in her room—her diary. I saw what she wrote."

I pulled out the black book and tossed it onto the desk. Yesterday I went back into Selena's room and grabbed the diary. I had been rereading it, hoping to find something about why she did this.

My brother appeared confused. "Diary? Did you allow her to bring it here?"

I shook my head. "Someone must have given it to her. I thought perhaps it was you since you were helping her."

He shook his head. "I didn't meet her until Italy."

I scratched my head. "The entries go back to the day I brought her here. The only people she came in contact with were Ricco and Ms. Marta."

Elba nodded and left the room. I knew he was going to get Ms. Marta to find out where that diary came from. Since they killed Ricco in Italy, there was no way of knowing if he gave it to her.

A few minutes later, Elba appeared. "I can't find Ms. Marta."

I blinked. Now that I thought about it, I noticed I wasn't served breakfast today. "I think she gave it to Selena." I swallowed.

Elba's eyebrows shot up in surprise. "What makes you say that?"

"I didn't receive my breakfast today; Ms. Marta always brings it to me. And Ricco has been with our family since Angel was still alive, whereas I hired Ms. Marta only weeks before Selena came here."

Elba nodded slowly. "Can I see the diary?"

I handed it over to my brother.

He flipped the pages and, after a minute, came over to my side. "You see this last page?" He pointed. "The ink is the same, but the penmanship is different. Not drastically different that anyone would notice, but look at the *e's* and *g's*. They're more angled on the last entry. I think someone else wrote it."

I plucked the book from my brother's hand and scrutinized the words. "I think you're right."

I still was unsure, but with Ms. Marta suddenly missing, I felt like this was much bigger than Selena running off. I knew the Dratshevs were involved, but why did they involve Selena?

Chapter 18

S elena

Five days.

That was when I last saw Domenick. I cursed myself for ever thinking he'd hurt me. I was an idiot to believe he was using me. And three days ago, I left the message with Domenick like my mom wanted. I fought and fought against it, but Marko's men had tortured me so much, I finally gave in.

Now I knew what real torture meant—my mother made sure of that.

Since I left the message on Domenick's phone, Marko had moved me from that first room. Instead of sleeping on the urine-soaked couch, I now had a bed—though I think that had more to do with the men complaining that when they assaulted me, the room smelled like piss.

My mother told them they could do whatever they liked to me, except for rape, and that was only because she didn't want me to get knocked up. She complained about how she hated babies.

I reminded her how I was a baby once. She just stared at me and said, "I know."

I rarely slept now, too afraid to close my eyes. But when I slept, I dreamt of Domenick. Of the way he touched me. How he swore to protect me and never left my side when I was shot.

"Where is she?" I heard my mom yell outside my room.

They had moved me into their apartment. From what I had learned over the last several days, Marko owned the building.

"I'm not my sister's keeper," Marko roared.

The man yelled all the time. I didn't think I had ever heard him speak in a normal tone. When he did lower his voice, it was the most evil and menacing sound I have ever heard.

Domenick wasn't the devil. Marko was.

"Look at this mess," my mom yelled back.

I heard feet stomp across the floor, and suddenly, my door flew open.

"Selena," my mom sneered at me. "It's time to earn your keep. Clean up the kitchen and make us lunch."

I rolled my eyes. "That's okay; I'm fine here." She never liked it when I talked back.

She folded her arms over her chest. "No wonder I left you."

I stood and pushed my hands onto my hips. "If I was so awful, why did you wait until I was twelve? Why not leave once I was born?"

"It's not like there were a lot of men lining up to be with a woman who just gave birth. It wasn't until I heard about Angel taking over the neighborhood that I knew there was someone worthy of my time."

I frowned. "So, you did what you always do. You lied and pretended to care, when, really, you were only using him for his money... just like you did with Dad."

She shrugged. "Dad was a step up from where I came from, but it was an accident. I got knocked up by him, and he thought we should get married."

Dad was a good guy. It was too bad my mom was the worst person ever.

As I walked past my mom, she grabbed my arm and pulled me back toward her. "I'm warning you, if you don't start pulling your weight around here, I'll make sure you're not so comfortable anymore."

I snorted. This was her idea of comfortable?

I tried to yank away from her grasp, but it only tightened. "What do you want from me?" I shouted.

If she wanted me dead, then I would have been killed by now. She wanted something from me, but what?

"What do I want?" she scoffed. "I want you to earn your place here. I want you to be useful for once in your life."

As if she was ever around to notice what I did.

I looked around the dingy apartment and at the men lounging on the couches. "And what are they useful for?"

She smirked. "They're useful for keeping the money flowing. And you," she pulled me closer, "you're useful for keeping them happy. Once Domenick is taken care of, I'll get you fixed so there's no way you can ever get pregnant. Then you'll be real useful."

I felt a wave of nausea wash over me. My mom wanted me to be a prostitute for Marko's men.

"I'm not a dog."

She smirked. "No, you're not, Selena. At least dogs are cute."

As my mom walked away, I couldn't help but wonder if Domenick was looking for me. I had to believe he was still out there, searching. I couldn't let go of that hope.

As I left my room, I walked through the living room, which was filled with thick clouds of smoke from the cigarettes and cigars the men were smoking. I began cleaning the small, dingy kitchen. The counters were stained, and the appliances were outdated. The floor was grimy, and there were roaches scurrying around.

My mind wandered to the last time I saw Domenick. He had promised to always protect me, and I had believed him.

"Where have you been?" my mom yelled from the living room.

"Grocery shopping," a female responded, though I hadn't heard her voice before. Maybe because this was the first time my mom had let me out of my room.

"I had to get Selena to clean up your mess, Nat."

I tried to lean closer to the doorway to hear their conversation, but they must have moved into another room.

I took out all my anger from the past five days on the grime that coated the kitchen.

"Wow. It actually looks good in here."

I was so focused on scrubbing the sink that I hadn't realized someone had walked into the kitchen. I gasped and turned. "Oh, you scared me." I clutched my chest.

The woman was tall, slender, with a long blond braid. "Sorry." Her lips thinned, and she reached out her hand. "I can take over now."

"Are you their maid?"

Her gaze fluttered to the ceiling. "Seems like it, huh? Nope, I'm Marko's sister, Nat."

"You clean for your brother?"

"It's not like I have a choice. No one chooses who they're related to."

I looked behind her at my mother, who was speaking to a man on the couch. "Truth," I mumbled under my breath. "So, your brother uses you to be his maid, and my mom uses me to, uh... pimp me out."

Nat frowned. "Is that what..." She lowered her voice and came closer to me. "Is that what's happening? I knew you were being held here, but I didn't know she was making you..." Her words drifted away as if she was going to be sick.

I nodded slowly, tears welling up in my eyes. "Yeah, she wants me to be a prostitute for Marko's men. And she wants to get me fixed so I can't ever get pregnant."

Nat's face twisted in disgust. "That's sick. You don't deserve any of this, Selena."

What she said surprised me.

"I never told you my name."

"I heard my brother and your mom talk about you."

That made sense. I had been here five days, after all.

"I just want to get out of here and warn Domenick about my mom."

Nat's eyes softened. "I wish I could help you, but—"

"Nat, make us lunch. And this time, don't burn the dessert," Marko called out.

Nat winced. She stood there, staring at the floor. They had hurt her too. It wasn't just being forced to clean for her brother, it was something else as well.

There may be a chance I could escape one day from this prison, but Nat was tied to Marko for the rest of her life.

"I can help you." Reaching over, I squeezed her shoulder lightly. "I'm pretty good at cooking, especially baking."

The look she gave me was a mix of hope and uncertainty. "My brother is very particular about what he eats. A man in his position has to be careful about who cooks for him, ya know?"

I got it.

"I'll just do the dessert, okay? You don't even have to tell them I made it."

She nodded. "It would help me a lot. I'm not very good at cooking, and even worse at baking."

We chuckled, and I opened the cabinets to find food to use. They had typical baking supplies like flour and sugar, but then I saw the bowl of apples in the corner and got an idea.

"Do they like apple pie?"

"It's actually Marko's favorite."

I smirked. "My dad's too. I'll get started on the pie, and you cook." Turning toward her, I grabbed her hand. "I promise that when I get out of here, I'm taking you with me."

Nat frowned. "My brother may not live lavishly like the Satrianos, but don't mistake that for being less ruthless. This is my life, Selena. I stupidly thought I had a way out, but I learned to never rely on someone else to save you."

My heart ached for Nat, but I meant what I said. There was no way I'd leave her behind.

"We're having a special guest for dinner." My mother strolled into the kitchen. "Your aunt, Nat."

My mouth fell when I saw who was at her side. "Ms. Marta?" I blinked in shock.

"Hello, Selena." Ms. Marta smiled at me, but it wasn't her usual caring grin. This one sent a cold shiver down my back.

"Hi, Aunt Marta," Nat said.

God, I remembered Ms. Marta trying to drug me with the apple, but I had no clue she was a Dratshev.

My mom sneered at me as she guided Ms. Marta back to the living room.

"Fuck," I whispered to myself. "Did you know she was in Domenick's home? Working as his cook."

Nat wouldn't look at me. "I knew my brother had planted her inside, but I didn't know anything else. Look, I have tried to escape so many times, and I really thought I had an out the last time. My family is awful, but the Satrianos aren't much better."

Maybe Nat had a point. Maybe there was no escape from these families.

I opened the spice cabinet and scanned the bottles. My eyes widened when I saw the bottle I was hoping for, and I clutched the spice to my heart. "Perfect. Now I can make my pie."

Chapter 19

D omenick

"Five fucking days," I growled like a rabid dog.

Because that was exactly how I felt. Wild. Enraged. Cornered.

It had been five days since Selena went missing, and I had nothing.

"No one is talking. Even Ms. Marta's scent went cold." Elba ran his hands through his hair.

"Didn't you mention you had a contact with the Dratshev family? Their maid or something like that?"

Elba turned his head and walked over to the French doors that looked out over the back garden. "Not anymore."

I watched as Elba stood with his back to me, his broad shoulders tensed like a coiled spring. It was strange seeing him like this. He was usually so focused and on top of things, but Selena's disappearance had clearly gotten to him. I took a step toward him, my hand reaching out to comfort him, but he spun around before I could touch him.

"Don't." His voice was low and dangerous. "You can't just snap your fingers this time and everything will magically be okay. This is real life, and in real life, shit happens." He strode back over to me, his eyes blazing. "Five days and we have nothing. No leads, no suspects, nothing. Vitale, Iggy, and even Luca have nothing. I'm sorry, Domenick, but even I'm at a loss."

I nodded, feeling an icy knot of fear settle in my stomach. Elba was right. I was so used to taking control and making everything better, keeping everyone safe. But this time, nothing worked.

I looked out the window, noticing the bright sun above the trees. I had been up for days, searching for any clue that could lead us to Selena, but I couldn't even tell what time of day it was anymore.

All our efforts had been in vain. I didn't know what to do next. I was running out of time, and Selena's life was hanging by a thread.

I took a deep breath and looked at Elba. "We can't give up now. We have to keep searching. There must be something we missed."

Elba gave me a wry smile. "I knew you'd say that. But we've checked every inch of this city and talked to every person connected to the Dratshev family. There's nothing left to do."

My head fell as the realization hit me hard. "Let them have her. She doesn't want me, anyway."

I read those words in her diary. Even if Ms. Marta had planted that last page, Selena let her feelings be known on the previous pages. The only reason she stayed after Italy was because she was frightened.

My brother turned to me and placed his hand on my shoulder, but I shrugged it off. "What? Domenick, it isn't like you to let someone go."

"I was foolish to think I could win Selena's affection. Fuck. I don't even know why I'm telling you this..."

"Because I'm your brother; I'm *family*. If you can't talk to me, who then?"

"I first found out about Selena when her mother started dating Angel."

My brother's eyes widened in surprise, but he said nothing.

"I knew Eeva was up to no good, but when Angel wound up dead and she disappeared, I vowed I'd get my revenge. And so, I set my sights on Selena. I'd use her to trick Eeva into coming to me, and then I'd do to her what Eeva did to Angel. And once Selena gave me a baby, I'd get rid of her too."

My brother scratched his head. "But how could you have known Selena's father would come to you?"

"I had watched him for some time and knew he wasn't good with money. It was only a matter of time before he came to me.

I also planted one of my people next door to them, who kept an eye on Selena and her father."

I left out the part where I had been watching Selena too. The more I saw of her, the more I questioned killing her.

"So when did you decide it was time to take Selena?"

"When it was time to pay up. He came to me for money because the neighbor suggested me when the landlord screwed him over."

"That landlord sounds like a piece of work."

"I know. When I paid a visit to Selena's neighbor so he could drop my note to Mr. Alba in his mailbox, I found out what the landlord had done to Selena."

My brother only nodded. He knew not to ask questions about what the landlord did to Selena. He knew what that meant.

"I went to visit the landlord, preparing to kill him right then, but the slimy bastard begged for his life by giving me information. He told me Selena and Rohon were preparing to run, which I already knew. I let him think I wouldn't kill him. He took me to surprise Mr. Alba, and that's when I removed the landlord from Selena's life forever. And I made it obvious that Selena would be wise to do as I said."

He smirked. "You're my brother, and I love you. Now tell me when your plan turned from revenge to love."

I chuckled. "Am I that obvious?"

My brother nodded. "I've never seen you so protective of a woman. And it wasn't just that. The way you cared for her, sat by her bedside every day and night when she was hurt. You love her."

I rubbed my forehead. "I shouldn't. As head of the family, it puts us at risk—"

"You're allowed to fall in love, Domenick. And Selena is a wonderful woman."

"But it's obvious she doesn't love me."

I'm just a monster in her eyes.

"I don't believe that's true." He glanced out the window and sighed. "I'm sure at first, she hated you. Hell, there are still times I hate you." My brother chuckled. "But when she looks at you now, since we've come back from Italy, that's love. She would never have left you willingly; they kidnapped her. I've watched her since she's been out of bed. There were so many times she could have escaped, and she didn't. She wants to be here. She wants to be with you."

Maybe my brother was right. I thought about it for a minute and decided it was time for me to take a risk. In the past, I always made sure I got what I wanted. I may have been able to put my life at risk, but never my heart.

Now, it was time to take a risk for Selena. Even if my brother was wrong, Selena was worth saving.

I shook my head. "There's one more person we need to talk to again. Selena's father."

Elba smiled. "So, we're going after her?"

I nodded.

"Good. Whether or not you believe me, Domenick, you deserve happiness."

"Maybe, but let's focus on coming up with something else to get Selena back. Nothing has worked up to this point."

"I know you think he has something on Eeva, but her father would have told us by now."

"I know, but there's something else. He's hiding something, and I don't think it is Eeva," I said, my mind racing with plausible scenarios.

Elba stood and grabbed his gun from the table. "Alright, let's go."

I did the same, feeling a sense of purpose for the first time in days.

We made our way out of my office and up to Mr. Alba's room. Upon opening the door, I found him with his head in his hands on the couch.

The curtains were closed, and the room was dimly lit. We cautiously made our way into his bedroom and found Rohon sobbing. His clothes were crumpled, as if he had been seated in the same spot for a long time.

When he glanced up, he looked exhausted and beaten down, like he hadn't slept in days. "Have you found her?" His voice was hoarse.

"No, that's why we're here," I said, coming to stand in front of him. "Is there anything you aren't telling us? Remember, your daughter's life is at stake."

"I'm a coward," he mumbled.

"That's not an answer," Elba said.

Rohon rubbed his eyes. "No, it's not. And this isn't the life I pictured for my daughter. What happens when I tell you the truth, Mr. Satriano? You get her back, sure. But then what? She's just a pawn in your sick game."

I should have been angry; I should have grabbed him and threw him against the wall to demand answers. But I wasn't angry, and I wouldn't grab him and demand answers. He cared for her as much as I did.

He never wanted her involved. He loved Selena. My father never loved me, and I stupidly thought Selena's father was using her too. That he didn't love her.

"I'm sorry." My voice was low. "You're right, Mr. Alba. She was a pawn, and I had planned on killing her."

"No."

"But then I fell in love with her. She has my heart, whether she knows it or not. If I kill her, I kill my heart. I protect those I love, but I'd die for Selena."

Rohon stared up at me for a moment, unmoving, before he muttered, "I never thought I'd say this, but I believe you. You truly love my daughter."

"I do," I replied, my voice sincere.

161

He nodded, wiping his face with his sleeve. "I'm sorry for any role I may have played in this mess. I just wanted to provide for my daughter."

"I want what's best for her too. That's why I need to know everything."

He sighed. "When you showed up at my home and took Selena, I was desperate to get her back. I thought you were going to do unspeakable things to her."

He wasn't wrong. That was my plan, but plans change.

"Then Eeva reached out to me. She wanted to meet on the south side in a dingy apartment. I thought she had fallen on hard times, but she told me there was a guy who could help. His name was Marko Dratshev."

My brother and I looked at each other.

"That's who we think has Selena," my brother said. "Can you tell us where this apartment is located?"

Selena's father was silent for a moment. "She lied about so many things... Eeva promised to keep her safe, but she lied. Mr. Satriano, Eeva's not a good woman. Believe nothing that comes out of her mouth."

"I know. I've seen what she can do. But if we have an address, we can save Selena from her mother."

I ran as soon as Selena's father finished telling us the address.

Chapter 20

S elena

I stood in the kitchen doorway, watching my mother dab the corners of her mouth with the cloth napkin.

"At least you didn't burn it this time," she sneered at Nat.

That was the difference between Nat and me. She was allowed to eat at the table, but I could only eat in my room. But my mother realized I was in the kitchen helping Nat, and I would be useful in serving dinner.

So, here I stood, watching them eat delicious meat and potatoes in a butter sauce, while my mother drank white wine and the men drank beer. My stomach rumbled as I watched, my mouth salivating. I hadn't eaten a decent meal in almost a week, and it was starting to show. I was so tired all the time, even after

I slept all night. Baking the dessert took so much out of me that all I wanted to do was head back to my room and lie on my bed.

"Don't worry, Selena. Whatever we don't eat, you can have." My mom smiled and raised her glass to me as if I were the guest of honor.

Ms. Marta, who sat on the other side of my mom, smiled. I frowned as I watched the women I thought were good and caring bond over their mutual evil. I wanted to walk over and slap that glass out of my mom's hand, then shove Ms. Marta's face into her plate of food. But I clenched my jaw and kept my mouth shut.

I had to bide my time until I could escape. And if everything went right, in about an hour, I'd be out of here.

"You did good tonight, Nat. Now for dessert," Marko barked.

Nat stood, almost knocking her chair back. "I, uh... I made apple pie."

"Sounds good," one of the other men at the table said.

Everyone seemed happy, except for my mother. She was smarter than them, which I hoped wouldn't be a problem.

"I never remember you making that before." My mother narrowed her eyes at Marko's sister. "You always make cookies... *burnt* cookies."

"I thought I would try something different." Nat stared at the floor, looking completely guilty.

Fuck. She's going to screw it all up.

My mother tilted her head, leaning in for the kill. "But why?"

I glared at Nat, hoping she'd remember what I said.

"The store. They had, uh... a sale on apples. I bought an apple pie mix and some pre-made crust. It seemed like a good idea at the time." Nat stood there, refusing to look at my mother.

My mother's brow rose. "A sale? Huh. Okay."

I let out a breath. My god, it actually worked.

One of the few things I remembered about my mom was her attraction to sales. If something was on sale, then she'd buy it whether we needed it or not.

Nat nodded and came back into the kitchen. I stepped aside and pointed to the individual plates. "Take these. I'll help dish them out."

She nodded, and I got busy plating the apple pie. And right before I was about to dish up the piece for my mom, I glanced back out into the dining room.

My mother's lips were pursed as she watched everyone get served. She was still suspicious, and I had to make a choice. Closing my eyes, I sucked in a breath before letting it out.

I served up the last two plates—one for my mom and one for Nat.

As she came back into the kitchen and scooped up the plates, I said, "These are for you and my mom. This one is—"

"Nat, what's taking so long? It's just pie," my mom shouted.

"Don't worry, Selena. I remember what you told me." She winked and scurried back out to the dining room.

Shit. I had changed it and didn't have time to tell her.

I had come up with a plan that I would use all the nutmeg in the apple pie because too much was poisonous. Since I didn't know how much each person would get in a slice, I hoped I used enough to at least make everyone sick.

But I made a smaller pie for Nat—one that didn't have any nutmeg in it. I had told her my plan, and she agreed to help.

Only, once I knew my mom was suspicious, I changed the plans slightly.

"Selena, get out here," my mom called.

Did she know what had happened? Had Nat told her what we were planning?

I took a fortifying breath and made my way to the dining room table.

"Yes?" I gazed around the table. All the men were shoveling the pie in their mouths. I wanted to smile but kept my features under control.

"Everyone loves the pie, and I thought it would be a shame if you didn't try it." She held up her plate, then immediately snatched Nat's plate and placed it in front of her.

I swallowed and glanced down at Nat.

Her eyes were wide with worry. "Uh, Selena doesn't like apples. Isn't that what you told me in the kitchen?"

She was trying to help, but it only made my mom more suspicious.

"I don't care what she likes or doesn't like; she better learn to do what I say—something she was terrible at when she was little. Go on, Selena, take a bite of the pie."

I noticed a man wincing as he chewed. Was he already getting sick?

I had to eat the pie fast. I not only took a bite, but I shoved the whole slice into my mouth.

My mother frowned, and Nat gasped. I chewed and chewed, almost choking, but I got the food down my throat.

"I may not have liked you, Selena, but I never thought you were a pig. Ugh, that was disgusting." My mom frowned, though she took her fork and ate her first bite of pie. "It is delicious, Nat. You surprise me. No wonder Selena was such a disgusting pig about it."

I stood there and watched as my mother ate the entire thing.

"More," Marko called out as he held up his plate.

Nat scurried to her feet and ran into the kitchen with his plate, and I quickly followed.

Once we were in the kitchen, she grabbed my arm and pulled me over to the sink. "Selena, you throw that up now. Please."

"It's okay. I switched plates. I knew my mom would either switch plates with you or make one of us eat from her plate first. So, the nutmeg-free pie was on her original plate."

Nat's eyes widened. "But you didn't tell me that. I almost started eating the pie."

"I was trying to tell you before you went out with the plates, but you ran off."

Nat clasped her chest. "I really thought you had poisoned yourself."

Right at that moment, there was a loud bang.

"What was that? It didn't sound like it came from the dining room," I said.

We went to the doorway and saw everyone get up from the table. My mom screamed as gunfire erupted and ran toward the bedrooms.

We ducked back into the kitchen and crouched down. Panic set in when we heard yelling and fighting in the other room. I knew we had to get out of there, but we were trapped. The only way out was through the dining room, and that was where the men were gathered.

I looked around the kitchen, searching for anything we could use to defend ourselves. My eyes landed on the oven. "Grab some oven mitts," I said to Nat as I opened the door and pulled out the baking sheet. It was still hot from baking the pie, but that was exactly what I needed.

I handed one mitt to Nat and kept the other for myself. We made our way to the doorway, ready to fight if we had to. I took a deep breath, ready to charge into battle.

But the scene before us stopped me in my tracks. The men were all lying on the ground, their weapons scattered around them. My mother was the only one not in the room.

When I glanced up, my heart leapt. It was Domenick.

"Selena. Are you okay?" He ran over, and I dropped the pan. I wrapped my arms around him before I could answer. "Yes, now that you're here." Tears welled in the corners of my eyes.

"What happened?" he asked.

I pulled back and tilted my head. "What do you mean? Didn't you shoot them?"

"No. We were about to, but then they all grabbed their stomachs and hunched over. A few vomited, and then they all seemed to pass out at once."

I stepped back and looked over at Nat. "It worked... The nutmeg worked."

She nodded, but I noticed one of Domenick's men had grabbed her by the arm and was dragging her away. "Don't hurt Nat. She helped me." I tried to go after her, but she was dragged out of the apartment.

"She's a Dratshev, Selena."

I folded my arms. "We can't choose our family, Domenick. They treated her like a servant. She's their sister, and she was being used to cook and clean for them."

Domenick looked around and sighed. "I won't kill her, okay? I can promise you that."

After what I had been through the past several days, I would not back down. "You won't do anything to her. She never wanted to be a part of this. She risked her life to help me." I waved at the groaning Dratshev men on the floor.

A man came up and whispered in Domenick's ear. He nodded as the man walked off.

"We'll discuss it later. Right now, we found your mother. Do you wish to save her too?" He folded his arms, ready to fight me, but for my mom, I had no fight left.

"No." I looked over his shoulder to see Elba come out from the back hallway, pulling my mom by the arm. She had vomit dribbling down her chin and looked like she wanted to pass out.

Her eyes fluttered up to mine, and that was when I said it loud enough for her to hear: "It you wish to behead my mother, Domenick, then do it. She's nothing to me; I have no mother."

"I was hoping you'd say that." He took a deep breath, and, instead of turning toward my mother, he said, "There's something I need to tell you, Selena. I knew your mother; I knew her when she first left you and your dad."

My heart raced as I stared up at Domenick in shock. "What do you mean? How could you know my mother?"

"My father wasn't a good man, and he abused all my brothers relentlessly. And when he turned on my youngest brother, Luca, I tried to protect him, but I failed." Domenick sighed.

I reached up and touched his cheek. I couldn't imagine the horrors he had to endure.

"My father always blamed Luca for my mother's death, and what he did to us was nothing compared to what he did to Luca. One day, I stopped my father."

He was silent for a moment, and I understood. It seemed my mother was telling the truth about Domenick killing his father, but I didn't blame him, and it didn't make him a monster. If anything, it made him a loving and protective brother.

"That's when Angel took us in. He was like the father I had never had... the father I had always longed for." He turned to glare at my mother. "Until *she* entered his life. She ruined him. Nearly destroyed his business, and then she stabbed him in the back, killing him."

I gasped. "You killed him?" I knew my mom was a terrible person, but I hadn't realized she resorted to killing.

"He was going to break up with me, Selena," my mother slurred. "I couldn't let that happen. It was because of Angel that I ended up with low-life thugs like Marko."

I covered my face, ashamed to be related to this woman. Once I lowered my hands, I nodded. "Now I know why you were after my father. You wanted to hurt her through him or me. You thought she'd hear I was taken and come begging for me. But you didn't realize how horrible my mother truly is."

"Yes. I had been planning this for a long time, Selena. But the more I watched you from a distance, the more intrigued I was by you. I had wanted to kidnap you and, I'm ashamed to say, kill you. But over time, I wanted to marry you. And I made up so many excuses in my head as to why I should marry you, and none of them was the truth—which is that I love you."

171

My eyes widened, and I took a step back. His jaw ticked as nothing came out of my mouth.

Domenick took a step closer and reached out to touch my arm. "I know it sounds crazy, and maybe it is, but I can't help how I feel about you, Selena. I know I have no right to ask this of you, but please... marry me. I'm not forcing you to do it. If you don't want to marry me or see me ever again, I'll let you walk out that door. I'll never come for you or your father."

He was letting me go. I got my wish, to be free from the Devil. My shoulders sank as I realized he never was the devil in the first place.

"I love you, Domenick."

His eyes brightened.

"This is strange and not at all how I pictured a proposal would look like." I gazed around the room at all the sick people around me—even my mom had passed out.

"I love you, Selena." He was about to grab my hand but stopped himself. "But if you want to leave, you can. You deserve love that isn't forced, love that blooms from your heart."

I smiled and stepped forward, cupping his cheek. "Then I'm just a rosebud, and you're my sunshine."

Domenick's lips turned up into a grin, and he leaned down to kiss me. It was soft, like a butterfly landing on a flower.

I felt a sense of peace wash over me as we pulled away. I had finally found someone who loved me for me, and not for what I could offer them.

"I'll marry you, Domenick, but on one condition."

He raised an eyebrow, waiting for me to continue.

"That you let Nat go."

He groaned but nodded. "Anything for my little dove."

Chapter 21

Domenick

It had been a week since I found Selena at the Dratchevs'. A week since she finally said yes to my proposal—I had stayed true to my word and kept Nat safe—and I couldn't wait to make her my wife.

Apparently, she couldn't wait either, because she agreed to marry me today.

"There's still time to run," Elba whispered in my ear.

I pulled on the lapel of my tuxedo jacket and shook my head. "Never. Nothing could take me away from this moment." I stared down the dirt path covered in pink rose petals, between the rows of white folding chairs, waiting for my bride to appear.

Selena insisted we get married in Florence. The wedding was outside in the garden of a grand estate a connection of ours owned.

She wanted to come back to Italy and make wonderful memories here. It was when she suggested the location that I got an idea for her wedding gift.

"Is the honeymoon all arranged?" I asked my brother.

"Yes. It's on a hill overlooking the countryside."

I nodded. "We will spend our honeymoon there. Do not disturb us. That means you're in charge for the next week."

"Of course."

I heard the soft rustling of leaves and the faint sound of birds singing in the distance as Selena appeared at the end of the path. She looked absolutely stunning in her cream silk wedding dress, glowing in the sunlight. My heart skipped a beat as she started making her way toward me, her eyes locked with mine.

As she got closer, I could see the slight tremble in her hands and the tears in her eyes. I reached out and took her hand, giving it a loving squeeze. "You look beautiful," I whispered, leaning in to kiss her cheek.

Selena smiled, her eyes shining with happiness. "Thank you, my love. You look pretty handsome yourself."

I couldn't help but feel a rush of emotions as we stood in front of the priest. This was it, the moment I had been waiting for my entire life. To spend the rest of my days with the woman I loved more than anything in this world.

I was so focused on Selena that I almost missed when the priest asked if I'd take Selena as my wife.

I smiled down at my beautiful bride. "I do."

"Do you, Selena, take Domenick Anthony Satriano as your loving husband?"

Her lips trembled, but she didn't say a word. For a moment, I thought she had changed her mind. I gazed out on the crowd and noticed even her father looked concerned.

But then, just when the silence became unbearable, Selena spoke up. "I do," she said, her voice strong and resolute. The relief that flooded me was immense. I wanted nothing more than to spend the rest of my days with this woman by my side, and I now knew she felt the same way.

As the ceremony continued, I found myself lost in a daze of happiness and love. The words of the priest washed over me in a blur, my eyes never leaving Selena's face. She was my world now, and I would do anything to make her happy.

The moment came when we were declared husband and wife. I leaned in to kiss Selena, sealing our vows with a passionate embrace. The guests erupted into cheers, and I couldn't help but smile as we made our way back down the aisle.

As we walked hand in hand toward our reception, I felt a sense of elation. This was it. Selena was officially family.

Once we were inside the large tent and greeting guests, Selena screamed.

My heart raced as I scanned the tent. What was happening? I turned to look at Selena to see if she was hurt, and there was a huge grin on her face.

"Camela! Oh my god, you came." Selena was jumping up and down, holding a woman's hand.

"Of course I came! I wouldn't miss my bestie's wedding." The woman had shoulder-length, fiery red hair. "And when you told me what happened when you called, I had to meet the man who literally stole your heart."

Selena introduced me to her friend. Camela cracked a few jokes and worried Vitale might like her. I made a mental note to tell Selena to keep Camela away from my brother.

Because I worried my brother would break her heart.

The celebration was in full swing as the day went on. The music was playing, the champagne was flowing, and everyone was dancing. Selena and I shared our first dance as husband and wife, our bodies swaying to the romantic melody of Frank Sinatra's "Fly Me to the Moon." She felt so warm and soft in my arms, and I felt like the luckiest man in the world. I knew I would do whatever it took to make sure she felt loved and cherished every single day of our lives together.

But as the sun started to set, I noticed Selena's eyes drooped with exhaustion. I realized just how much stress and pressure the wedding had put on her, and I knew we needed some alone time.

"Excuse us for a moment," I said to our guests, taking Selena's hand and leading her out of the tent and into the cool night air.

We walked in silence for a few moments until we found ourselves in a secluded corner of the estate's gardens. I turned to look at Selena, taking in her beauty in the moonlight.

"Are you okay?" I asked her softly, brushing her hair back from her face.

She nodded, leaning into my hand. "I'm just tired. It's been a long day."

"Then I think it's time to exchange our gifts to each other." I smiled and kissed the back of her hand.

Her face lit up. "Let me run and get your gift. I hope you like it." She scurried off, and I chuckled.

This must be what contentment felt like.

Once I made my way back into the tent, Elba told me the car was waiting to take us to our honeymoon location.

I found Selena, and we made our way outside to the waiting car. The air was crisp and cool, the stars twinkling above us. I helped Selena into the car, then got in beside her. The driver closed the door, and we were off.

She lifted a box wrapped in golden paper. I pulled it apart and saw a black box. Once I opened it, I smiled. "A watch." My brows rose. "You have good taste."

She pointed at the watch. "It's gold, so I knew you'd like it."

Leaning over, I kissed her cheek. "I love it."

She watched me slip it on my wrist. "And mine?" she asked.

I sat back and stared out the front windshield into the moon-lit night. "I didn't get you a watch."

She groaned. "I didn't think so, but you got me something. I mean, since you bought my dad that condo back in Chicago, I figured my gift would, well... be something."

I tried holding back my laughter as I watched her squirm. "You'll get it when we stop."

The cute little wrinkle between her brow appeared. "Okay." She tried to play it cool, but I noticed her leg bounce in antici-pation.

The car finally came to a stop, and Selena practically leapt out the door. She gazed around as if she knew what she was looking for.

"How do you like it?" I came around the black sedan and wrapped her in my arms as the driver pulled around back.

"Is this where we're staying for our honeymoon?"

"Yes, but it's also your wedding present."

Her eyes widened, and she turned around, taking in the large, two-story Italian villa. It was painted a deep terracotta color, and the roof was made of rustic red tiles. A large balcony jutted out over the front door.

She clasped her chest and stared. "It's gorgeous."

"And it's all yours. Anytime you want to come here, you just say the word, and this is where we'll live."

She turned to me with tears in her eyes. "Domenick, I don't know what to say. This is the most amazing gift anyone has ever given me."

I hugged her tightly. "You deserve it, Selena. You deserve everything, and I want to give it all to you."

She looked up at me, her eyes shining with unshed tears. "I love you so much, Domeniak."

"I love you too, Selena," I said, leaning down to kiss her.

As we walked into the villa hand in hand, I knew this was just the beginning of our lives together. And I couldn't wait to see what the future held for us.

Chapter 22

S elena

 I inhaled. The scent of flowers filled the air. A warm, light breeze tickled my skin. The sun was setting, painting the sky a vibrant orange and red. "This place is beautiful."

A month after leaving Florence and almost being killed, I was back. But this time, I was on my honeymoon.

Thoughts of the wedding yesterday and Domenick swirled in my head. I had never been happier than I had been the last few days.

The wedding was everything I had ever dreamed, and even Camela came. It was fun catching up with her. She told me how amazing my life sounded, and that she'd love to have the adventures I had over the past month.

I shook my head. It had only been a month since I first met Domenick, but it felt like I had known him forever.

I wanted him to take in the beautiful view from our villa in the country. Once I told Domenick the Dratshevs' driver had tricked me by telling me he was taking me to his villa, Domenick thought it would be a good idea to get a villa for real.

So, he bought me a villa in the Florence countryside as a wedding present.

While I loved the gift, I felt like my present for him was inadequate.

"I bought it for you. You deserve only the best," Domenick said, walking into the bedroom and over to the small balcony where I stood.

I gasped as he pulled me into his arms from behind. "It's too much. Gifting my father that new condo that overlooks Lake Michigan and now this villa... It's so—"

He cut me off by turning me and kissing my lips. As he lifted his head, he said, "I could buy you the world, and it wouldn't be enough. I could capture the universe and all the stars, and it would be nothing compared to my love for you."

Heat traveled up my cheeks. I leaned my head on his chest.

Domenick's arms tightened around me. He looked down at me with a soft smile. "I want to make you happy," he whispered, his breath tickling my ear. "And I want to spend the rest of my life with you."

My heart swelled with happiness. I had never felt so loved and cherished by anyone before. Domenick was perfect for me in every way.

I looked up at him and smiled. "I love you."

He grinned, his eyes sparkling with love. "I love you too."

We stood there for a moment, basking in the warmth of each other's love, before Domenick leaned down to kiss me again. This time, his kiss was more urgent, his fingers tangling in my hair.

I moaned softly, my body responding to his touch. He lifted me up and carried me to the bed, laying me down gently. He unbuttoned his shirt, and I wanted to help him. He was my husband now, and I wanted to please him. I sat up, my hand sliding over the silky golden bedspread.

As I reached for him, he grabbed my wrist. "No. You're my wife, and it's my job to please you." He leaned down and kissed me deeply, his lips and tongue exploring my mouth. I moaned again, my body arching up to meet his.

Domenick's hands roamed over my body, his touch setting me on fire. As he slowly removed my clothes, he whispered the most beautiful things into my ear, his breath hot and heavy. I shivered with pleasure and anticipation.

When I was completely naked, Domenick took off his clothes. Once he was done, he lay down beside me, stroking my hair. "You're so beautiful," he breathed. "I can't believe you're mine."

I blushed, feeling both embarrassed and thrilled. Domenick was the first man to make me feel truly beautiful and desired.

He leaned down to kiss my neck, his lips and tongue trailing down to my breasts. I sucked in a breath as he took one nipple into his mouth, nibbling on it until I was writhing with pleasure.

He moved his frame over mine and languidly made his way down my body until he was dotting kisses between my thighs. I gasped as his tongue flicked over my clit. He gripped my thighs as he licked me, his tongue sliding over me.

I grabbed his hair, trying not to hold back my moans as my body tensed with the overwhelming sensations racing through me. Domenick's tongue never stopped moving, his eyes locked on mine. He lowered one hand and slid a finger inside me, and I groaned when another finger joined the first.

"You're so wet," he said before sliding his fingers inside me. Then his tongue moved over my clit, stroking it gently. My body tensed, my eyes slamming shut as a powerful orgasm overtook me.

"I'm coming!"

He may not have known me long, but Domenick knew how to touch me.

I was still reeling from the orgasm when he pushed himself over me, his cock sliding inside me easily. I wrapped my legs around him as he thrust into me, moaning softly.

I was still sensitive from my climax, but Domenick's cock inside me just made the orgasm last longer. My body tightened around his cock. Domenick groaned as his fingers slid over my ass and circled my puckered hole.

I nibbled on my lower lip and whispered, "Yes."

He had done that a few times before, and I found I loved it when he filled me. It always made my orgasms more intense.

He wiggled his finger until it pushed inside my asshole. There was a slight burn, but it soon faded into something otherworldly.

My arms slipped from the hold I had on him. My muscles turned weak as he fucked me in both holes.

"Fuck, Selena. I can already feel you tightening on my cock."

I felt complete with him inside me, and my world faded as he rammed into me. I loved the feeling of his cock sliding in and out of me. His thrusts became faster, his cock pounding into me. I moaned, my body writhing against his.

"You're so perfect and tight," he whispered into my ear. "I never want to stop fucking you."

I squeezed my eyes shut. "Oh, god," I cried as the pressure inside me continued to build. I wanted to stay like this forever.

"I'm coming." I wrapped my arms around him, my fingers digging into his back.

The orgasm was so intense, I cried out his name. Stars exploded behind my eyes, and I heard Domenick call my name.

When I came to, Domenick was looking at me with soft eyes, and I could see how much pleasure he felt from how they were shining.

He kissed me, and I could taste myself in his mouth. He rolled off me and got up to go into the ensuite bathroom.

After a few moments, he came back with a damp washcloth. He took his time cleaning me up and taking care of me before he slid next to me.

"I love you," he whispered as he pulled me against him.

I sighed as I snuggled into his embrace. I drifted off to sleep knowing I was loved and protected. With Domenick at my side, I'd be happy for the rest of my life.

Chapter 23

D omenick

"Everything smells delicious." I wrapped my arms around my wife as she stirred the sauce.

She smiled and leaned her head back onto my chest. "I know Elba likes my simple spaghetti and tomato sauce, so I thought I'd make it for lunch."

I dotted kisses down her neck. We came back from our honeymoon a week ago. Since we got married, life had been better than I could have ever imagined. And since I executed Marko, Eeva and the rest of the Dratshev family in Chicago, I felt like my life was perfect.

"And for dessert, I made apple pie," she said with a wink as I pulled away and leaned against the counter next to her.

"Not too much nutmeg this time." I chuckled.

She reached up and caressed my cheek. "Only extra nutmeg for unwanted guests."

I grinned at her, feeling incredibly lucky to have Selena by my side. Everything about her made me feel complete—her smile, her touch, her voice, and the way she moved every inch of her body made my heart skip a beat. We had gone through so much together, yet our love had only grown stronger with time.

Someone cleared their throat, and I looked toward the entrance of the kitchen. There stood Elba, his face emotionless. He used to smile so much more, but since Selena entered our lives, I noticed his happiness fading.

I hated to even think about it, but maybe my brother was jealous of what I had with Selena.

"Right on time. The sauce is done. You two take a seat. I put out some freshly-made garlic bread for you two."

I waved for my brother to take a seat at the kitchen table. Once we were seated, Selena came over with large bowls filled with spaghetti and sauce. She then grabbed the block of parmesan and grated it over our dishes. "I'll leave you two to your meal. I'm taking my dad to lunch in the city." She blew a kiss at me, and I smiled, watching her exit the kitchen.

My brother started twirling his spaghetti-filled fork around in his spoon. "So, how's married life treating you?"

I smiled. "Better than I could have ever imagined. Selena's the best thing that's ever happened to me."

Elba nodded, taking a bite of his food. After he swallowed, he said, "I'm glad to hear that. You deserve to be happy."

I frowned. "What's been bothering you, Elba? You seem distant lately."

He put his fork and spoon down. "It's about Selena."

I knew he was jealous.

"Look, you'll find someone too, Elba—"

"I have found someone. Only, she wasn't who she said she was." He leaned back in his chair.

"What? Who's this woman?"

Elba folded his arms over his chest and glanced out the French doors. "That's why I wanted to talk to you today. I need to leave the family... I need to leave and never come back."

I put down my utensils. "Leave? Are you that unhappy with us?"

My heart sank as I stared at my brother, unsure of what to say. I had never seen Elba like this before. No matter what happened to our family, I could always count on Elba being there, but now he seemed lost and defeated.

"It's the woman I met... She didn't just cause me pain; she hurt our family."

My mind raced with possible women he could be talking about. "Don't tell me it was Eeva."

"No, of course not. This woman may have fooled me, but I wasn't stupid enough to date the woman who killed Angel."

"Then who is this woman you're willing to leave the family for?"

"I'm not leaving the family for her; I'm leaving the family to pay for what she did."

I sat there, stunned, trying to make sense of what my brother was saying. "What did she do?"

"She's the reason Fern and Marko kidnapped Selena. She's the reason Marko knew you had Selena in Italy. This woman was the snitch, and she used me to get that information."

My heart stopped. I couldn't comprehend what my brother was saying. This couldn't be true. My brother couldn't have put our family at risk like that. He was the smartest guy I knew. How could a woman have tricked him?

My anger boiled over as I stood up from my chair. "I thought that was Ms. Marta. Is it someone else?"

Elba hesitated. "It was Natassia Dratshev."

"Marko's sister?" I coughed on my words.

Elba nodded. "Yes, Marko's sister."

I clenched my fists, feeling nothing but rage and betrayal. How could Elba have been so foolish to fall for Natassia's lies? And to think Selena made me let her go...

"How could you be so foolish as to trust any Dratshev? I don't care if she's the most beautiful woman alive and sucked your cock until you saw angels floating above. *Never trust a Dratshev.*"

I never wanted to let Natassia go, but I loved Selena and promised her. Selena swore Natassia helped her, but maybe that was a trick too.

Elba stood, his fist clenched. "It wasn't like that, Domenick. She wasn't like that."

My brows shot up. "Apparently, it was like that. She didn't seem to mind hurting your family. What made you think getting in bed with a Dratshev was a wise move?"

He rubbed his brow. "I didn't think, okay? When we met, I didn't know who she was... It doesn't matter. The point is, I'm sorry. I know what you do to snitches, and I know you wouldn't hesitate to kill me."

My stomach rolled, and I pushed Selena's delicious food aside. He was right. I had to kill my brother. It wasn't so difficult to pull the trigger on my father, but that was because he was a monster.

But Elba was no monster. He was a guy who got seduced by the wrong woman.

"I'll make it easy on you, Domenick." My brother stared straight ahead, refusing to look at me. "I'll disappear. Do what you want to Natassia; I don't care. And, if you find me, then you can kill me too. Just, uh... just give me a bit of a head start, okay?"

To anyone else, I'd take the gun out of my holster and shoot him dead before he even finished his speech. But this was Elba.

He was only a year younger than me. He was my best friend... if someone like me could even have a best friend.

My throat tightened. What was I going to do?

Either way, I would lose him forever.

"I'll give you one day. Just, uh... stay away from me and my family. If you talk to anyone, I'll know."

"Got it," Elba turned to leave.

"Elba!"

He turned around. "Yeah?"

"We were close once, and that's why I'm giving you this one chance. If I find you, I will kill you."

Elba nodded and left.

I knew the fairytale of the last week wouldn't last. And when I found Elba, that was when the fairytale would be destroyed for good.

Epilogue

Selena

I watched Domenick as he sipped his espresso and stared out the French doors to the back garden. He hadn't been himself since Elba left last week.

He wouldn't tell me why Elba disappeared, but I heard from Vitale that Elba got tangled up with the wrong woman—someone Domenick wouldn't approve of.

I hated that he was fighting with his brother.

But then I got a surprise. And I wanted to share it with Domenick and hoped it would put a smile on his face.

"Here you go. One freshly baked bun." I placed the white ceramic plate in front of my husband.

"What is this? I don't eat pastries in the morning. Are you testing out a new recipe?"

I nibbled at my lower lip. "No. I just thought it would make you happy."

A wrinkle appeared between his brow as he glanced down at the baked good and then back up at me. "What type of bun is it?"

"I don't know." I shrugged, trying to swallow the laughter as he appeared even more confused.

"But you made it. Why don't you know what type of bun it is?"

"I didn't make it alone... *you* helped."

He sighed and stood. "Selena. Are you feeling alright? I didn't help you make anything..." His words slowly died on his lips as what was happening sank in. "Wait. Are you telling me you're pregnant?"

I nodded, tears of joy streaming down my face as I reached for Domenick's hand. He stared at me, his eyes wide with shock, and then a smile slowly spread across his face. He pulled me into his arms, lifting me off the ground and twirling me around before setting me back down.

"I can't believe it," he whispered, his lips brushing against my temple as he held me close.

"I know. Neither can I," I admitted, feeling overwhelmed with emotion.

Domenick pulled back, cupping my face as he gazed into my eyes. "You've made me the happiest man alive, Selena. We're going to have a baby."

I laughed, tears still streaming down my face as I leaned in to kiss him. It was as if a weight had been lifted off Domenick. The sadness that had been clouding his eyes was now replaced with a newfound happiness.

"We are," I confirmed, my hand resting on my stomach.

He leaned down and kissed me. A deep, fiery passion ignited between us. It was as if we were newlyweds again, filled with excitement and anticipation for the future.

Domenick's hands explored my body, sending shivers down my spine. I moaned into his mouth, wanting more of him.

As we pulled away, he leaned his forehead against mine, his breath hot against my skin. "Selena, I have to tell you something." His voice was serious, and my heart skipped a beat.

"What is it?"

"I want you right now, right here." His gaze drifted to my belly. "Can we still have sex with your... condition?"

I giggled. "Of course we can. As much as you want." I winked at him.

Domenick's eyes lit with desire as he picked me up and placed me on the kitchen island. He trailed kisses down my neck and chest, his hands running over my not-yet-growing belly. I moaned and leaned back on my arms, arching my back.

"I love you, Selena," he whispered, looking up at me with a mixture of adoration and lust.

"I love you too, Domenick," I replied, reaching for him and pulling him closer.

He lifted my skirt and pulled down my panties, then he lowered to his knees. Leaning in, he kissed the apex of my thighs.

He touched my clit with his tongue, sending a jolt of electricity through me. My pussy was already wet, my need for him building as his fingers explored me.

"Oh! Domenick..." I moaned, pulling his hair. He groaned in response, sending vibrations through my clit.

Domenick plunged his tongue into me, licking me up and down as I bucked against him. His thumb pressed against my nub as he continued to lick me. I fisted his hair, pulling at his head. I was so close to orgasm, but Domenick wouldn't let me come.

He pulled away, leaving me panting, my hips quivering.

"Domenick..." I moaned, trying to get him to continue. He smiled, knowing how aroused I was.

He undid his belt and lowered his pants, and his cock sprang free. Then he pulled my hips toward him, spreading my legs.

He entered me, his movements slow and deliberate at first, teasing me even more. But his pace quickened as his need grew, and we lost ourselves in the moment.

It was as if nothing else in the world mattered except for the two of us and the life growing inside me.

He slid his thumb over my clit as he pushed in and out of me. "Fuck. You feel so good, Selena."

It wasn't long before I felt my climax build into something powerful. He flicked my clit once more, and it sent me over the edge.

I moaned loudly, my hips bucking against his. Domenick grunted, his orgasm close. I felt his familiar warmth enter me.

"I love you, Selena," he whispered, grinding his cock against my clit as he came.

Only this time, it felt even better. He pulled out of me, spilling his seed all over me. I quivered as I watched him, and then I collapsed back on the island.

"Domenick..." I whispered, and he lifted his gaze to mine. His breath was still coming out in long huffs, his eyes still glistening with lust.

I reached up and ran my fingers through his hair, pulling him down for a kiss. He playfully bit my lower lip, and I giggled against his mouth.

"Whatever happens, know I'll always protect you and the baby."

"You'll be the best dad."

A softness crossed his features—an expression I had only witnessed a few times. It was his love for me, but now amplified to include our little one.

I had never felt so cared for in my life, and I couldn't wait to raise this baby with him.

The End

About Josie Max

Josie Max is the second pen name for a USA Today Bestselling author. When she's not writing romance books she loves to spend time with her two boys, drink coffee, and indulging in chocolate (a little too much).

Find out more about Josie Max on her website: www.josie maxwrites.com

Made in the USA
Monee, IL
18 July 2023

Made in the USA
Monee, IL
18 July 2023